Pippi in the South Seas

Astrid Lindgren

Translated by Marianne Turner
Illustrated by Tony Ross

OXFORD
UNIVERSITY PRESS

OXFORD
UNIVERSITY PRESS

Great Clarendon Street, Oxford OX2 6DP

Oxford University Press is a department of the University of Oxford.
It furthers the University's objective of excellence in research, scholarship,
and education by publishing worldwide in

Oxford New York

Auckland Cape Town Dar es Salaam Hong Kong Karachi
Kuala Lumpur Madrid Melbourne Mexico City Nairobi
New Delhi Shanghai Taipei Toronto

With offices in

Argentina Austria Brazil Chile Czech Republic France Greece
Guatemala Hungary Italy Japan South Korea Poland Portugal
Singapore Switzerland Thailand Turkey Ukraine Vietnam

Oxford is a registered trade mark of Oxford University Press
in the UK and in certain other countries

First published as *Pippi Langstrump I Söderhavet* by Rabén & Sjögren 1955
First published in this edition 2006

British Library Cataloguing in Publication Data available

All foreign and co-production rights shall be handled by Kerstin Kvint Agency AB,
Stockholm, Sweden

ISBN-13: 978-0-19-275481-3
ISBN-10: 0-19-275481-5

10 9 8 7 6 5 4 3 2

Typeset by AFS Image Setters Ltd, Glasgow
Printed in Great Britain by
Cox & Wyman Ltd, Reading, Berkshire

Contents

1. Pippi Still Lives at Villekulla
   Cottage   1
2. Pippi Cheers up Auntie Laura   14
3. Pippi Finds a Squeazle   22
4. Pippi Arranges a Quiz   32
5. Pippi Receives a Letter   43
6. Pippi Goes Aboard   50
7. Pippi Goes Ashore   58
8. Pippi Reproves a Shark   66
9. Pippi Reproves Jim and Buck   75
10. Pippi Gets Tired of Jim and Buck   88
11. Pippi Leaves Canny Canny Island   94
12. Pippi Longstocking Does
    not Want to Grow Up   101

1
Pippi Still Lives at Villekulla Cottage

T he tiny little town was looking very trim and cosy with its cobbled streets, its small, low houses surrounded by little gardens. Everyone who came there thought it must be a very quiet and restful town to live in. But there were not many places of special interest to a visitor—only one or two: and these were a folk museum and an ancient burial mound; that was all. Oh no!—there was just one other thing. The people in the little town had put up neat notice-boards which clearly marked the way for those who wanted to see the sights. On one of them it said in large letters: 'To the Folk Museum', and underneath there was an arrow to show the way; on another it said: 'To the Long Barrow'.

But there was still one more notice-board. It said:

To Villekulla Cottage

It had been put there recently because people kept asking the way to Villekulla Cottage—as a matter of fact, far more often than they asked the way to the folk museum or the long barrow.

One beautiful summer's day, a gentleman came driving into the little town in his car. He lived in a much bigger town; that was why he had got it into his head that he was better and more important than the people in the tiny little town. Of course, there was this about it, too, that he had a big, shining car, and he himself looked very imposing with his highly polished shoes and with a fat gold ring on his finger. It was hardly surprising, then, that he thought himself exceedingly grand and superior.

He honked loudly as he drove through the streets of the little town to make sure that people would notice him.

When the fine gentleman caught sight of the notice-boards he laughed scornfully.

' "To the Folk Museum"—'pon my word!' he said to himself. ' "To the Long Barrow"—I say, how *exciting*!' he jeered. 'But what nonsense is this?' he said, when he caught sight of the third notice-board. ' "To Villekulla Cottage". What a name!'

He thought for a moment. An ordinary cottage can hardly be a show-place like a folk museum or a long barrow. The board must have been put up for some other reason, he thought. Finally, he came to the conclusion, The house must be up for sale, and the board has been put there to show the way for prospective buyers. The fine gentleman had intended, for some time, to buy a house in a small town where life would be quieter than in the big city. Of course, he would not live there all the time, he would only visit it now and then when he wanted a rest. Besides, in a small town it would be more noticeable what a particularly fine and grand gentleman he really was. He decided to go and look at Villekulla Cottage at once.

He had only to follow the direction in which the arrow was pointing. The road took him to the very outskirts of the little town before he found what he was looking for. There, on a very ramshackle garden gate, was printed in red crayon:

VILLEKULLA COTTAGE

Behind the gate he saw an overgrown garden and old trees covered with moss, uncut lawns, and masses of flowers growing exactly as they liked. At the far end of the garden there was a house— but, oh dear, what a house! It looked ready to fall down at any minute. The fine gentleman stared at it, and suddenly he gave a gasp. *There was a horse standing in the porch.* The fine gentleman was not used to seeing horses in porches. That was why he gasped.

On the steps of the porch, in the brilliant sunshine, sat three little children. The one in the middle was a girl with a lot of freckles on her face and two red plaits which stuck straight out. A very pretty little girl with fair curls, and dressed in a blue-checked cotton frock, sat on one side of her, and a little boy with neatly combed hair on the other. A monkey crouched on the red-haired girl's shoulder.

The fine gentleman thought he must have come to the wrong place. Surely no one would expect to sell such a ramshackle house.

'Look here, children,' he shouted, 'is this miserable hovel really Villekulla Cottage?'

The girl in the middle, the one with the red hair, rose and walked towards the gate. The other two followed slowly.

'Answer me, can't you?' said the fine gentleman irritably, while the red-haired girl was still approaching.

'Let me think,' said the red-haired girl, frowning thoughtfully. 'Is it the folk museum?—No! The long barrow?—No! I've got it!' she shouted. 'It's Villekulla Cottage!'

'Answer me properly,' said the fine gentleman, getting out of his car. He had decided to look at the place more closely in any case.

'Of course, I could pull it down and build a new house,' he muttered to himself.

'Oh, yes, let's start straight away,' cried the red-haired girl, quickly breaking off a couple of planks from the side of the house.

The fine gentleman did not listen to her. Small children were of no interest to him, and besides, now he had something to consider. The garden, in spite of its neglected state, really looked very pleasant and inviting in the sunshine. If a new house were built, the grass cut, the paths raked and beautiful flowers planted, then even a very fine gentleman could live there. The fine gentleman decided to buy Villekulla Cottage.

He looked round to see what further

improvements might be made. The old mossy trees would, of course, have to go. He scowled at the gnarled oak tree with a thick trunk. Its branches stretched right over the roof of Villekulla Cottage.

'I'll have that cut down,' he said firmly.

The pretty little girl in the blue check dress cried out.

'Pippi, did you hear?' she called in a terrified voice.

The red-haired girl took no notice and practised hop-scotch on the garden path.

'That's it—I'll have that rotten old oak tree cut down,' said the fine gentleman to himself.

The little girl in blue looked at him imploringly.

'Oh, please don't,' she said. 'It's—it's such a good tree for climbing. And it's hollow. You can sit inside it.'

'Nonsense,' said the fine gentleman. 'I don't climb trees. You should know better than that.'

The little boy with the tidy hair also came forward. He was looking worried.

'But,' he pleaded, 'ginger-beer grows in it. And chocolate, too—on Thursdays.'

'Look here, children, I think you've been sitting out here too long and have got a touch of the sun,' said the fine gentleman. 'But that's no concern of mine. I'm going to buy this property. Will you tell me where I can find the owner?'

The little girl in the blue check started to cry, and the boy ran to the red-haired girl who was still practising hops.

'Pippi,' he said, 'can't you hear what he's saying? Why don't you do something?'

'Do something?' said the red-haired girl. 'I keep hopping as if my life depended on it, and then you come and tell me to do something. Try it yourself and see how *you* get on.'

She went over to the fine gentleman.

'I'm Pippi Longstocking,' she said, 'and this is Tommy and Annika.' She pointed at her friends. 'Can we help you in any way? If there's a house to be pulled down, or a tree to be pulled up, or anything else to be altered, you have only to say so!'

'Your name does not interest me,' said the fine gentleman. 'All I want to know is where I can find the owner of this house. I'm going to buy it.'

The red-haired girl, the one whose name was Pippi Longstocking, had gone back to her exercise.

'The owner is otherwise engaged at the moment,' she said. She hopped with great concentration while she spoke. 'Extremely engaged,' she said, hopping round the fine gentleman. 'But won't you sit down a moment, and I'm sure she'll come?'

'She?' said the fine gentleman, pleased. 'So it's a she who owns this miserable dwelling? All the better. Women don't know anything about business matters, so I may get the whole lot for a song.'

'Let's hope so,' said Pippi Longstocking.

Since there did not appear to be anywhere else to sit, the fine gentleman placed himself cautiously on the porch steps. The little monkey jumped nervously to and fro on the veranda railing. Tommy and Annika, the two charming and well cared for children, stood some distance away, looking at him anxiously.

'Do you live here?' asked the fine gentleman.

'No,' said Tommy, 'we live next door.'—

'But we come here every day to play,' said Annika shyly.

'I'll soon put a stop to that,' said the fine gentleman. 'I won't have any children running round my garden: there's nothing worse.'

'I quite agree,' said Pippi, who stopped hopping for a moment. 'Children ought to be shot.'

'How can you say such a thing?' said Tommy in an injured voice.

'What I mean is that all children *ought* to be shot,' said Pippi. 'But it wouldn't do, because then there would never be any kind old gentlemen. And we couldn't do without them, could we?'

The fine gentleman looked at Pippi's red hair and decided to pass the time by teasing her.

'Do you know what you have in common with a newly struck match?' he asked.

'No, I don't,' said Pippi, 'but I've always wanted to know.'

The fine gentleman tugged quite hard at one of Pippi's plaits.

'They're both flaming at the top,' he said, roaring with laughter.

'I wonder I didn't think of that before,' said Pippi. 'We have to hear a lot before our ears drop off.'

The fine gentleman stared at her.

'I do believe you're the ugliest child I've ever seen,' he said.

'Maybe,' said Pippi, 'but it seems to me you're no oil painting yourself.'

The fine gentleman looked offended, but made no reply. Pippi watched him in silence for a time, her head on one side.

'Do you know what we two have in common?' she said at last.

'No. Nothing, I should hope,' said the fine gentleman.

'Oh, yes,' said Pippi. 'We're both swollen headed . . . except me.'

A faint giggle was heard from the direction of

Tommy and Annika. The fine gentleman went red in the face.

'So you're impudent,' he shouted. 'We'll soon put a stop to that.'

He stretched out a fat arm to take hold of Pippi, but she instantly jumped to one side, and a second later she was sitting high up in the hollow oak tree. The fine gentleman's mouth dropped open with astonishment.

'And when are we going to start to put a stop to my impudence?' asked Pippi, making herself comfortable on a branch.

'I can wait,' said the fine gentleman.

'Good,' said Pippi, 'because I'm thinking of staying up here until the middle of November.'

Tommy and Annika laughed and clapped their hands. But that was not a very wise thing to do as it made the fine gentleman furiously angry, and since he could not get hold of Pippi, he seized Annika by the scruff of her neck and said:

'Then I'll give you a spanking instead. It seems you can do with it, too.'

Annika had never in all her life been smacked, and she cried out in her fright. There was a thud as Pippi jumped down from the tree. With one leap she reached the fine gentleman.

'Oh no, you don't,' she said. 'I won't waste

time fighting you, but I'm going to put a stop to your meddling once and for all.'

Without delay, she seized the fine gentleman about his fat waist and threw him up in the air, twice. Then she carried him at arm's length to his car and threw him into the back seat.

'I don't think we'll pull the house down till another day,' she said. 'You see, once a week I pull down houses, but never on Fridays, because then I've got the weekly turning-out to think of. So I generally vacuum the house clean on Fridays and pull it down on Saturdays. It's always best to have a routine.'

The fine gentleman struggled with great difficulty into the driving seat and drove off at high speed. He was both frightened and angry, and he was annoyed that he had not been able to speak to the owner of Villekulla Cottage, because he was very eager to buy the place and turn the horrid children out of it.

It was not long before he met one of the little town's policemen. Stopping the car, he called to the policeman:

'Could you help me find the lady who owns Villekulla Cottage?'

'With pleasure,' said the policeman. He jumped into the car and said:

'Will you drive to Villekulla Cottage?'

'She isn't there,' said the fine gentleman.

'Oh yes, she's sure to be,' said the policeman.

The fine gentleman felt safe with a policeman beside him, and he drove back to Villekulla Cottage, as the policeman had told him to do, because he wanted so very much to speak to the owner of the house.

'That's the lady who owns Villekulla Cottage,' said the policeman, pointing towards it.

The fine gentleman looked, put his hand to his forehead, and groaned. For, on the porch steps, stood the red-haired girl, that dreadful Pippi Longstocking, and in her arms she carried the horse. The monkey was sitting on her shoulder.

'Come along, Tommy and Annika,' shouted Pippi. 'Let's have a ride before the next perspective buyer comes.'

'It's *prospective* buyer,' said Annika.

'Is *that* . . . the owner of the house?' said the fine gentleman in a weak voice. 'But it's only a little girl!'

'Yes,' said the policeman. 'It's only a little girl—the strongest girl in the world. She lives there all alone.'

The horse, now carrying the three children on his back, came galloping up to the gate. Pippi looked down at the fine gentleman and said:

'It was good fun guessing riddles just now, wasn't it? I know another one, too. Can you tell me the difference between my horse and my monkey?'

The fine gentleman did not really feel like guessing any more riddles, but by then he was so afraid of Pippi that he dared not refuse to reply.

'The difference between your horse and your monkey?—I don't know, I'm sure.'

'No, it *is* rather a tricky one,' said Pippi. 'But I'll give you a clue. If you see them both under a tree and then one of them starts to climb it, it's *not* the horse.'

The fine gentleman trod on the accelerator and disappeared at top speed. He was never, never, seen again in the little town.

2
Pippi Cheers up Auntie Laura

One afternoon Pippi was walking in her garden while she waited for Tommy and Annika to turn up. But no Tommy came, and no Annika either; so Pippi decided to go and see what they were doing. She found them in the green creeper-covered arbour in their garden. But they were not alone. Their mother, Mrs Settergreen, was there, too, with a dear old lady who had come to see them. They were just having coffee. The children were drinking orange juice.

Tommy and Annika ran to meet Pippi.

'Auntie Laura's here,' explained Tommy. 'That's why we didn't come over.'

'She looks sweet,' said Pippi, peering through the leaves. 'I must have a chat with her. I love dear old ladies.'

Annika looked a little anxious.

'Per . . . per . . . p'raps you'd better not talk too much,' she said, remembering the time when Pippi had come to a coffee party and talked so much that Annika's mother got quite annoyed with her. Annika was so fond of Pippi that she did not want anyone to be annoyed with her.

'And why shouldn't I talk to her?' said Pippi, offended. 'I certainly shall. You simply *have* to be nice to visitors. If I sit here saying nothing, she may think I don't like the look of her.'

'But are you quite sure you know how to speak to an old lady?' Annika said doubtfully.

'You cheer them up, that's what you do,' said Pippi emphatically, 'and that's what I'm going to do.'

She went into the arbour. First she curtsied to Mrs Settergreen. Then, with raised eyebrows, she looked at the old lady.

'Well, and if it isn't Auntie Laura!' she said. 'Getting younger every day! I wonder if I might have a little orange juice so that my throat doesn't get too dry, just in case we should want to do some talking.'

The last remark was addressed to Tommy and Annika's mother. Mrs Settergreen poured out a glass of orange juice, saying, as she did so:

'Children should be seen and not heard!'

'Indeed!' said Pippi. 'People have both eyes and ears, I should hope; and though I'm certainly a pleasure to *look* at, it won't do their ears any harm to have a little exercise as well. But some people seem to think that ears are only meant for waggling.'

Mrs Settergreen did not take much notice of Pippi, but turned to the old lady.

'And how are you feeling these days?' she asked sympathetically.

Auntie Laura looked worried.

'Oh, not at all well, my dear,' she said. 'My nerves are very bad, and I get so anxious about everything.'

''Xactly like Granny,' said Pippi, vigorously dipping a biscuit in the glass of orange juice. 'Her nerves were very bad and the least little thing upset her. If she was walking in the street and a roof tile happened to fall on her head, she would start to jump and scream and make such a terrible fuss it made you think there had been an accident. Once she went to a ball with Daddy and they were doing square-dancing. Daddy is fairly strong, and all of a sudden he happened to send Granny flying right across the ballroom into the middle of the double bass. She immediately began to scream and make a fuss again. Then Daddy took hold of her and held her at arm's length out of the fourth-floor window, just to calm her down a little, so that she wouldn't feel nervous any more. But it didn't help! "Let go of me at once," she screamed. Daddy did, of course. But just fancy!—even then she wasn't satisfied! Daddy said he'd never known such a woman for getting excited about nothing. Yes! It must be dreadful to have an ache in the nerve,' said Pippi with feeling as she dipped another biscuit.

Tommy and Annika fidgeted uncomfortably on their chairs. Auntie Laura looked bewildered and Mrs Settergreen hastened to say:

'I do hope you'll soon feel better, Auntie Laura.'

'She will,' said Pippi encouragingly. 'Granny did. She got terrific'ly well, because she took something soothing.'

'What kind of thing?' asked Auntie Laura with interest.

'Fox poison,' said Pippi. 'A level tablespoonful of fox poison. It did the trick, because afterwards she sat dead still for five days and never said a word. Calm as a cucumber! Completely cured, in fact! No more jumping about and shouting. No matter how many tiles dropped on her head, she just sat there and enjoyed herself. So there's nothing to stop Auntie Laura getting well, because, as I said, Granny did.'

Tommy crept up close to Auntie Laura and whispered in her ear:

'Don't take any notice, Auntie Laura. It's just a story she's been making up! She hasn't got a granny.'

Auntie Laura nodded to show that she understood perfectly. But Pippi's ears were good, and she had heard Tommy's whisper.

'Tommy's right,' she said. 'I haven't got a granny. None at all. So what had she got to be so terribly nervous about?'

Auntie Laura turned to Mrs Settergreen.

'My dear, something *quite* extraordinary happened to me yesterday . . .'

'It couldn't possibly have been so extraordinary as what happened to me the day before yesterday,' Pippi interrupted. 'I was travelling by train, and while the train was going at top speed a cow came flying through the open window with a big suitcase hanging from her tail. She sat down on the seat facing me and began to turn the pages of the railway timetable to find out when we were supposed to arrive at Hayfield junction. I was just eating my sandwiches—I had tons of sandwiches with pickled herrings and sausages in them—and I thought maybe she was hungry, so I offered her one. She took a sandwich with pickled herring in it and ate it up.'

Pippi went silent.

'That was really most extraordinary,' said Auntie Laura kindly.

'Yes, cows like that don't grow on trees,' said Pippi. 'Fancy choosing a pickled herring sandwich when there were masses of sausage sandwiches to be had.'

Mrs Settergreen refilled the coffee cups and gave the children some more orange juice.

'What I was going to tell you, when we were interrupted by our little friend here,' said Auntie Laura, 'was about a strange meeting yesterday . . .'

'Talking of strange meetings,' said Pippi, 'I'm sure you'd be amused to hear about Agathon and Theodore. Once, when Daddy's ship sailed to Singapore, we needed a new mate. So we got Agathon. Agathon was two and a half yards tall and so thin that his joints rattled like the tail of an angry rattlesnake when he walked. His hair was black as a raven and reached to his waist. He had only one tooth in his mouth, but it was all the bigger for that, and it stuck out far below his chin.

Daddy thought Agathon was on the ugly side and at first would not take him on board, but then he thought Agathon might be a useful person to have in case he wanted to frighten any horses into a gallop. Later on, we arrived at Hong Kong. There, we needed another mate. So Theodore came. He was two and a half yards tall, had hair as black as a raven which reached to his waist, and one big solitary tooth in his mouth. Agathon and Theodore were really enormously alike. Especially Theodore. As a matter of fact they were as alike as twins.'

'That certainly was strange,' said Auntie Laura.

'Strange!' said Pippi. 'What was strange about it?'

'That they were so alike,' said Auntie Laura. 'Very strange, don't you think?'

'No,' said Pippi. 'Not at all. They *were* twins. Both of them. Right from the time they were born, even.'

She looked reproachfully at Auntie Laura.

'I really don't know what you mean, Auntie. Do you think it's worth while making a to-do because two poor twins are a bit alike? They can't help it. You may be certain, dear Auntie, that no one would willingly look like Agathon. Not like Theodore either, for that matter.'

'Very well,' said Auntie Laura. 'But why did you mention these strange meetings, then?'

'If I could just be allowed to get a word in edgeways at this party,' said Pippi, 'I'd tell you of some strange meetings. You see, both Agathon and Theodore were extremely pigeon-toed. At each step they took, the big toe of the right foot bumped into the big toe of the left one. If that wasn't a strange meeting I'd like to know what is. Certainly the big toes thought so.'

Pippi helped herself to another biscuit. Auntie Laura rose to leave.

'But, Auntie Laura, you were going to tell us about a strange meeting yesterday,' said Mrs Settergreen.

'I think I'll put it off till another time,' said Auntie Laura. 'When I come to think of it, it wasn't so very strange after all.'

She said goodbye to Tommy and Annika. Then she gave Pippi's red head a pat.

'Goodbye, my little friend,' she said. 'You were right. I think I'm better already. I feel much less nervous now.'

'I *am* glad,' said Pippi and gave Auntie Laura a hearty hug. 'D'you know, Auntie Laura? Daddy was quite pleased when we got Theodore in Hong Kong. He said now we could frighten exactly twice as many horses into a gallop.'

3
Pippi Finds a Squeazle

One morning Tommy and Annika came, as usual, bounding into Pippi's kitchen and shouted, 'Good morning!' But there was no answer. Pippi was sitting in the middle of the kitchen table with Mr Nelson, the little monkey, in her arms, and with a happy smile on her face.

'Good morning,' said Tommy and Annika again.

'Can you believe it?' said Pippi dreamily. 'Can you believe it was *me* that thought of it? Me, of all people, that made it up?'

'What is it you've made up?' asked Tommy and Annika both together. It did not surprise them in the least that Pippi had made something up—she was always doing it—but they wanted to know what it was. 'But what is it, Pippi?'

'A new word,' said Pippi, looking at Tommy and Annika as if she had only just caught sight of them, 'a brand new word.'

'What word?' asked Tommy.

'A really super word,' said Pippi, 'one of the superest I've ever heard.'

'Tell us!' said Annika.

'Squeazle,' said Pippi triumphantly.

'Squeazle?' repeated Tommy. 'What does it mean?'

'I only wish I knew,' said Pippi. 'All I know is that it doesn't mean a vacuum cleaner.'

Tommy and Annika thought for a moment. At last Annika said:

'But if you don't know what it means, it's not much use, is it?'

'No, that's just what annoys me,' said Pippi.

'I wonder who first decided what words should mean,' said Tommy.

'A lot of old professors, I suppose,' said Pippi. 'I must say, people are pretty queer! Think of the words they make up! "Basin" and "trowel" and "string" and things like that. It's a mystery where they get them from. But squeazle, which really is a good word, they simply leave out. Wasn't it lucky I thought of it! And I'm jolly well going to find out what it means, too.'

She thought for a moment.

'Squeazle! I wonder if it's the top of a blue-painted flagpole,' she said doubtfully.

'There aren't any blue flagpoles,' said Annika.

'No, that's true . . . Well then, I really don't know. Could it be the sound you hear when you walk in mud and it gets between your toes? Let's see how it sounds: "Annika was walking about in the mud, making the most wonderful squeazly sound." '

She shook her head.

'No, it won't do. It should be "making the most wonderful squelchy sound".'

She scratched her head.

'This is getting more and more mysterious. But whatever it is, I'm certainly going to find out. Perhaps they've got it in a shop. Let's go and ask!'

Tommy and Annika thought this was a good idea. Pippi went to find her suitcase which was full of gold coins.

'Squeazle,' she said. 'Sounds expensive. I think we'd better take a gold coin.'

So she got ready. As usual Mr Nelson jumped

on to her shoulder and Pippi lifted the horse down from the veranda.

'We'd better be quick,' she said to Tommy and Annika. 'We'll ride. Otherwise there may not be any squeazles left when we get there. I shouldn't be a bit surprised if the mayor had bought the last one already.'

When the horse went galloping through the streets of the little town with Pippi, Tommy, and Annika on his back, his hooves made such a noise on the cobbles that all the children of the town heard it and came running, because they were all very fond of Pippi.

'Pippi, where are you going?' they shouted.

'I'm going to buy squeazles,' said Pippi, holding in the horse for a moment.

The children stopped short and looked bewildered.

'Are they good to eat?' asked one little boy.

'I should jolly well think they are,' said Pippi, licking her lips. 'They're delicious. At least, it sounds as though they are!'

She jumped off the horse outside a sweet shop and lifted down Tommy and Annika. They walked in.

'I'd like a quarter of squeazles,' said Pippi, 'the scrunchy kind.'

'Squeazles?' said the pretty girl behind the

counter thoughtfully. 'I don't believe we've got any.'

'Oh, you must have,' said Pippi. 'I'm sure they've got them in all well-stocked shops.'

'But we've just run out of them, I'm afraid,' said the girl, who had never heard of squeazles, but did not like to admit that her shop was not so well-stocked as the others.

'Did you have them yesterday, then?' cried Pippi, eagerly. 'Please, please tell me what they looked like. I've never seen any squeazles in all my life. Did they have red stripes?'

The girl blushed prettily and said:

'I'm afraid I don't know what they are! In any case we haven't got them here.'

Very disappointed, Pippi walked out.

'Well, I've just got to go on hunting,' she said. 'I'm not going home without squeazles.'

The shop next door was an ironmonger's. An assistant bowed politely to the children.

'I want a squeazle, please,' said Pippi. 'But it must be the very best quality—the kind you kill lions with.'

The assistant looked artful.

'Let's see,' he said, scratching his head. 'Let's see!'

He went over to fetch a small garden rake and handed it to Pippi.

'Will this one do?' he asked.

Pippi looked at him indignantly.

'That thing is what the professors call a rake,' she said. 'But it so happens I want a squeazle. You shouldn't try to swindle an innocent little child!'

The assistant laughed and said:

'I'm afraid we haven't got one of those you ask for. Try the draper's at the corner.'

'The draper's,' Pippi murmured when they were out in the street. 'You can't get it *there*; that's one thing I'm quite sure about.'

She looked discouraged for a moment, but she soon brightened up.

'Perhaps, after all, squeazles is a disease,' she said. 'Let's go and ask the doctor!'

Annika knew where the doctor lived, because she had been to him for vaccination.

Pippi rang the bell. A nurse opened the door.

'Can I see the doctor, please?' said Pippi. 'It's a matter of life and death.'

'Follow me,' said the nurse.

The doctor was sitting at his writing desk when the children came in. Pippi went straight up to him, shut her eyes, and put her tongue out.

'Well, what's your trouble?' asked the doctor.

Pippi opened her bright blue eyes and drew in her tongue.

'I'm afraid I've caught squeazles,' she said. 'I itch all over and my eyes won't stay open when I'm asleep. Sometimes I hiccup, and last Sunday I didn't feel at all well after I'd swallowed a plateful of shoe-polish and milk. I eat quite well, but very often the food goes down the wrong way and then it's just wasted. It must be attacks of squeazles. And please tell me—is it infectious?'

The doctor looked at Pippi's rosy little face, glowing with health, and said:

'I think there's less wrong with you than with most people. I'm sure you don't suffer from squeazles.'

Pippi grabbed hold of his arm.

'But there *is* a disease called squeazles, isn't there?'

'No,' said the doctor, 'there isn't. But even if there was such a disease, I don't think it would attack you.'

Pippi looked depressed. She curtsied to the doctor and said goodbye, and Annika did the same. Tommy bowed. They trailed off to the horse which was waiting by the doctor's garden fence.

Not far from the doctor's there was a tall three-storeyed house. On the top floor a window was open. Pippi pointed at the open window and said:

'I shouldn't be at all surprised if the squeazle wasn't in there. I'll pop up and have a look.'

Hand over hand, she quickly swarmed up the gutter pipe. When she had climbed to the level of the window, she threw herself recklessly across and caught hold of the window ledge, heaved herself up, and thrust her head in.

Two ladies were sitting inside the room, talking. Imagine their surprise when a red head suddenly appeared above the window ledge, and they heard a voice say:

'Have you got a squeazle in here, by any chance?'

The two ladies started in alarm.

'Good gracious, child, what's that you're saying? Has one escaped?'

'That's just what I should very much like to know,' said Pippi politely.

'Oh dear, supposing he's under the bed,' shouted one of the ladies. 'Does he bite?'

'I think so,' said Pippi. 'It sounds as if he had hefty tusks.'

The two ladies clung to each other in fright. Pippi looked round the room with interest, but at last she said sadly:

'No, there isn't so much as a sniff of a squeazle here. Sorry to trouble you, but I thought I'd better just make sure as I was passing by.'

She lowered herself down the gutter pipe again.

'There isn't a single squeazle in this town, worse luck. Let's go home.'

When they reached the porch and jumped down from the horse, Tommy nearly trod on a small beetle which was crawling on the sandy garden path.

'Oh, careful, Tommy, there's a beetle,' shouted Pippi.

They all three bent down to look at him. He was very small. His wings were green and shimmered like metal.

'Isn't he pretty?' said Annika. 'I wonder what it's called.'

'It isn't a cockchafer,' said Tommy.

'Well, it isn't a may-bug, and not a stag-beetle either,' said Annika. 'I wish I knew what kind it is.'

A blissful smile ran over Pippi's face.

'I know,' she said. 'It's a squeazle.'

'Are you sure?' said Tommy doubtfully.

'Do you think I don't know a squeazle when I see one?' said Pippi. 'Did you ever see anything so squeazlish in all your life?'

Carefully she removed the beetle to a safe place where nobody could tread on him.

'My pretty little squeazle,' she said tenderly. 'I

knew I'd find one in the end. But it's rather odd, I must say. We've spent hours and hours hunting all over the town for a squeazle, and all the time he was right in front of Villekulla Cottage!'

4
Pippi Arranges a Quiz

One day the lovely long summer holidays
came to an end, and Tommy and
Annika went back to school again.
Pippi still thought herself clever enough without
going to school, and she made it quite clear that
she did not intend ever to put her foot inside
one—at least not until the time came when she
felt she *must* know how to spell the 'ea' sound in
'seasick'.

'But as I'm never seasick I shan't have to
bother about the spelling for a long time,' she

said. 'And if I do get seasick I shall have other things to think of than trying to spell it.'

'I don't suppose you'll ever be seasick,' said Tommy.

He was quite right. Pippi had sailed the oceans with her father before he became Cannibal King and before she settled at Villekulla Cottage. But she had never been seasick.

Sometimes Pippi rode over to the school and brought back Tommy and Annika. This pleased them very much. They thoroughly enjoyed riding, and there are certainly not many children who can go home from school on a horse.

'I say, Pippi! Do come and fetch us this afternoon,' said Tommy one day, when he and Annika were about to return to school after their lunch hour.

'Yes, please do,' said Annika, 'because it's today that Miss Rosenbloom is going to give prizes to good and diligent children.'

Miss Rosenbloom was a rich old lady who lived in the little town. She was not very free with her money, but once a term she came to the school with gifts for the children. Not for all of them—oh no! Only the very good and hard-working children received prizes. To find out which children were really good and hard-working, she first held long oral examinations.

This was why all the children in the little town lived in a constant state of terror. Every day, when they were supposed to be doing their homework and were thinking of something pleasanter to do instead, their mothers and fathers would say:

'Now, don't forget Miss Rosenbloom!'

It was certainly a terrible disgrace to come home to their parents and small brothers and sisters, on the day that Miss Rosenbloom had visited the school, without a penny or a bag of sweets, or even a vest. Yes, a vest! Because Miss Rosenbloom also gave clothes to the poorer children. But however poor you were, it made no difference if you could not give the right answer when Miss Rosenbloom asked how many inches there are in a mile. No wonder the children in the little town were terrified of Miss Rosenbloom. They were afraid of her soup, too! They knew that Miss Rosenbloom would have them weighed and measured to see if any of them appeared to have too little food at home. All the thin and weedy-looking children had to go every day to Miss Rosenbloom's house at lunch-time and eat a large plateful of pea soup. It would have been all right if there had not been a lot of horrid husks in the soup.

The great day had now come when Miss

Rosenbloom would visit the school. The lessons finished earlier than usual, and all the children gathered in the school yard. A big table had been placed in the middle of the yard, and at the table sat Miss Rosenbloom. She had two secretaries with her who wrote down everything about the children—how much they weighed, and whether they could answer the questions; whether they were poor and in need of clothes; how many marks they had gained for good behaviour; whether there were any younger brothers and sisters who also needed clothes. There seemed no end to the things Miss Rosenbloom wanted to know. On the table in front of her she had a box of money, many bags of sweets, and great piles of vests and socks and woollen pants.

'Now, children, you're all to stand in lines,' shouted Miss Rosenbloom. 'In the first line, those without any younger brothers and sisters—in the second, those with one or two brothers or sisters—in the third, those with more than two brothers and sisters.'

Miss Rosenbloom was very methodical. And, of course, it was only fair that children with many brothers and sisters at home should have larger bags of sweets than those with none.

And so began the examination. How the children trembled! Those who could not answer had to stand in a corner and later they would go home without a single sweet for their little brothers and sisters.

Tommy and Annika, of course, were very good at their lessons. But all the same, the bow in Annika's hair shook with nervous excitement as she stood in the row beside Tommy; and Tommy's face got whiter and whiter the closer he came to Miss Rosenbloom. When it was his turn to answer, there was a sudden upheaval in the line of 'children without brothers and sisters'. Someone was pushing from behind. It was none other than Pippi. She burst through the line and walked straight up to Miss Rosenbloom.

'Excuse me,' she said, 'but I wasn't here at the beginning. Which is the line for people without fourteen brothers and sisters when thirteen of them are naughty little boys?'

Miss Rosenbloom looked most disapproving.

'You may stay where you are for the time being,' she said, 'but I should imagine it won't be long before you will be joining the group of children in the corner.'

Then the secretaries had to take down Pippi's name, and they weighed her to see if she needed soup. But she was four pounds too heavy for that.

'No soup for you, my girl,' said Miss Rosenbloom sternly.

'What a lucky escape!' said Pippi. 'Now I only have to try and keep clear of the pants and vests, and then I'll be out of the wood.'

Miss Rosenbloom did not listen. She was turning the pages of the spelling book to find a difficult word for Pippi to spell.

'Pay attention, girl,' she said at last. 'I want you to tell me how you spell "seasick".'

'With the greatest of pleasure,' said Pippi. 'S-e-e-s-i-k.'

Miss Rosenbloom smiled sarcastically.

'Oh,' she said, 'the spelling book has different ideas.'

'It's jolly lucky, then, that you asked me how *I* spell it,' said Pippi. 'S-e-e-s-i-k, that's the way I've always spelt it and it never did me any harm.'

'Make a note of it,' said Miss Rosenbloom to the secretaries. Her mouth was set in a thin line.

'Yes, do,' said Pippi. 'Take down this extra good spelling, and make sure it's put into the spelling book as soon as possible.'

'Well now, my girl,' said Miss Rosenbloom. 'Tell me this. When did Charles I die?'

'Oh, dear me!' exclaimed Pippi. 'Is *he* dead now? It makes you sad to think of how many people pop off nowadays. And I'm quite sure it need never have happened if only he'd changed his shoes when they got wet.'

'Put it down,' said Miss Rosenbloom in an icy voice to the secretaries.

'Yes,' agreed Pippi. 'And write down, too, that it's a good thing to put leeches on the body. And before going to bed you should drink a little warm paraffin. It keeps you wide awake!'

Miss Rosenbloom shook her head.

'Why has the horse ridges on his molars?' she asked severely.

'But are you quite sure he *has*?' said Pippi doubtfully. 'You could ask him if you wanted to. He's standing over there,' and she pointed to her own horse which she had tied to a tree.

'Wasn't it lucky I brought him?' she said happily. 'Or else you'd never have found out why he has ridges on his teeth. Quite honestly, I haven't any idea and I'm not specially interested, either.'

Miss Rosenbloom's mouth was by now set in an even thinner line.

'This is outrageous,' she muttered, 'quite outrageous.'

'That's just what I think,' said Pippi, with great satisfaction. 'If I go on being as clever as this it doesn't look as if I should be able to avoid having a pair of pink woolly pants.'

'Put it down,' said Miss Rosenbloom to the secretaries.

'No, don't bother,' said Pippi. 'I'm not so very keen on pink woolly pants, but you can put me down for a large bag of sweets, if you like.'

'You shall have one final question,' said Miss Rosenbloom in a strangled voice.

'Go ahead,' said Pippi. 'I like this sort of quiz.'

'Do you know the answer to this?' said Miss Rosenbloom. 'Peter and Paul are to share a cake. If Peter gets a quarter of it what does Paul get?'

'A tummy ache,' stated Pippi. She turned to the secretaries. 'Take notes,' she said solemnly. 'Write down that Paul gets a tummy ache.'

By this time Miss Rosenbloom had had quite enough of Pippi.

'You're the most ignorant and unpleasant child I ever met,' she said. 'Go and stand in the corner at once and feel ashamed of yourself.'

Pippi stalked off obediently, but she muttered angrily to herself:

'It's not fair! I answered every single question!'

When she had walked a few steps she suddenly remembered something and quickly made her way back to Miss Rosenbloom.

''Scuse me,' she said, 'but I forgot to give you my chest measurement and altitude. Take notes,' she said to the secretaries. 'It's not that I want soup—far from it—but the book-keeping must be correct.'

'If you don't go and stand in the corner at once,' said Miss Rosenbloom, 'I know of one little girl who will soon have a good spanking.'

'Poor child,' said Pippi. 'Where is she? Send her to me and I'll defend her. Make a note of that!'

Pippi then went to stand with the children who were supposed to be ashamed of themselves. They were feeling far from happy. Many of them sobbed and wept with the thought of what their parents and their brothers and sisters would say when they came home without any money and without sweets.

Pippi looked round at the weeping children and swallowed once or twice. Then she said:

'We're going to have a quiz all on our own!'

The children cheered up a little, but they did not quite grasp what Pippi meant.

'Stand in two lines,' said Pippi. 'All those who know that Charles I is dead, stand in one line; and those who haven't yet heard that he is dead, stand in the other.'

But as all the children knew that Charles I was dead, there was only one line.

'This will never do,' said Pippi. 'There have to be at least two lines, or else it's not proper. Ask Miss Rosenbloom; she'll tell you.'

She thought for a moment.

'I know!' she said at last. 'All children fully qualified in pranks, line up here.'

'And who's going to be in the other line?' eagerly asked a little girl who would not admit that she was full of pranks.

'The other line is for those who are *not yet* qualified,' said Pippi.

At Miss Rosenbloom's table the examination was in full swing, and now and then a small, weepy child came slowly over to join Pippi's group.

'Now comes the difficult question,' said Pippi. 'Now we shall see if you've done your homework properly.'

She turned to a thin little boy in a blue shirt.

'Pay attention!' she said, imitating Miss Rosenbloom. 'Tell me the name of someone who's dead.'

'Old Mrs Pettigrew at No. 57.'

'Good!' said Pippi. 'Do you know of anyone else?'

No, he could not think of anyone. Pippi cupped her hands round her mouth and whispered loudly:

'Charles I, of course!'

After that, Pippi asked all the children in turn if they knew of anyone who was dead, and they all answered:

'Old Mrs Pettigrew at No. 57 and Charles I.'

'This examination is going better than I expected,' said Pippi. 'I've got just one more question. If Peter and Paul are to share a cake, and Peter blankly refuses to eat more than one measly little quarter of it, who will then have to sacrifice himself by golloping all the rest?'

'Paul,' shouted all the children.

'My goodness! There can't be many children as clever as you,' said Pippi. 'You shall have your reward.'

And out of her pocket she brought handfuls of gold coins and gave one to each child. Then they each received a large bag of sweets which Pippi took from her rucksack.

And so it happened that there was great joy among all the children who had been put in the corner. When Miss Rosenbloom had finished her examining and it was time for everybody to go home, there were none who ran faster than those who had stood in the corner. But first, they all came up to Pippi.

'Thank you, dear Pippi,' they said. 'Thank you for the money and the sweets.'

'Oh, that's nothing,' said Pippi. 'You needn't thank me for *that*. But don't ever forget that I saved you from pink woolly pants.'

5
Pippi Receives a Letter

The weeks went by and soon it was autumn. Then autumn was over and winter followed. It was a long and cold winter which seemed as if it would never end. Tommy and Annika had to work very hard at school, and each day that passed they felt more and more tired and found it harder and harder to get up in the morning. Mrs Settergreen began to get quite anxious about their pale cheeks and their poor appetites. Then, on top of it all, both of them caught measles and had to stay in bed for two weeks.

These two weeks would have been very dull if Pippi had not come each day and done acrobatics outside their window. The doctor had forbidden her to go into the sickroom because of the risk of infection. Pippi obeyed, although she claimed she could undertake to squash one or two billion measle germs with her nails in an afternoon. But nobody had forbidden her to do acrobatics outside the window. The nursery was on the second floor, so Pippi had set up a ladder against the window. It was very exciting for Tommy and Annika, lying in their beds, to try and guess what Pippi would look like when she appeared at the top of the ladder, because she never looked the same two days running. Sometimes she was dressed as a chimney-sweep, sometimes as a ghost in a white sheet, and sometimes she was a witch. On other days she would act amusing plays outside the window, taking all the parts herself. Now and then she did physical exercises on the ladder—and *what* exercises! She would stand on one of the topmost rungs and let the ladder sway backwards and forwards, so that Tommy and Annika screamed with fright and thought she would tumble down at any moment. But she never did. When she wanted to climb down to the ground she always went head first just to make it more amusing for Tommy and Annika to watch. Every day she went into the town and bought apples and oranges and sweets. She put them all in a basket and tied a long string to the handle. Then she sent Mr Nelson up with the end of the string to Tommy, who opened the window and hauled up the basket. Sometimes Mr Nelson brought a letter from Pippi when she happened to be busy and could not come herself. But that was not often, because Pippi spent nearly all day and every day on the ladder. Sometimes she pressed her nose against the window pane and turned her eyelids inside out and made the most horrible faces. She told Tommy and Annika that they would each have a gold coin if they did not laugh, but it was quite impossible not to do so. Tommy and Annika laughed so much they nearly fell out of their beds.

By and by, they got well and were allowed up. But—oh, how thin and pale they were! Pippi sat with them in the kitchen on their first day up and watched them eating porridge. That is to say, they were supposed to be eating porridge, but they were not getting on with it at all well. Their mother felt really anxious when she saw them pecking at their food.

'Eat up your lovely porridge,' she said.

Annika stirred the porridge round in her plate, but she could not bring herself to swallow even a spoonful.

'*Why* must I eat it?' she asked plaintively.

'*What* a silly thing to ask,' said Pippi. 'Of course you must eat your lovely porridge. If you don't, you won't grow big and strong. And if you don't grow big and strong you won't be able to make *your* children one day eat *their* lovely porridge. Oh, no! Annika. Think of the dreadful muddle there would be over the porridge-eating in this country if everyone talked like that.'

Tommy and Annika ate two spoonfuls of porridge each. Pippi watched them sympathetically.

'What you need is a sea voyage,' she said, rocking her chair to and fro. 'That would soon teach you to eat. I remember once, when I sailed in my father's ship, that Fridolf, one of our sailors, suddenly found he couldn't eat more than seven platefuls of porridge for breakfast. Daddy nearly went out of his mind with worry over Fridolf's poor appetite. "My dear Fridolf," he said, almost in tears, "I am very much afraid that you are suffering from a wasting disease. I think you'd better stay in your bunk today until you feel better and can eat like other people. I'll come'and tuck you up and give you some strengthening meducin!" '

'It's *medicine*,' said Annika.

'And Fridolf tottered off to bed,' continued Pippi, 'because he was worried himself, and wondered what terrible plague had struck him so that he could only manage seven platefuls of porridge. He was lying in his bunk wondering if he would live till nightfall when Daddy brought the meducin. It was a black, nasty meducin, but say what you will about it—it was certainly strengthening.

'As soon as Fridolf had swallowed the first spoonful a flame of fire seemed to shoot out of his mouth. He shouted so loudly that the *Hoppetossa* shook from bow to stern and they could hear it on ships fifty sea-miles away. The cook hadn't cleared away the breakfast things yet when Fridolf came up from his cabin, steaming, and uttering loud roars. He threw himself down at the table and began to eat porridge, and after the fifteenth plateful he was still calling for more. But there was no porridge left, and the only thing the cook could think of was to keep throwing cold boiled potatoes into Fridolf 's open mouth. The moment the cook looked like stopping Fridolf growled angrily, so the cook knew he'd have to go on, if he didn't want to be eaten up himself. But unfortunately he had only got a mere 117 potatoes, and when he had thrown the last one into Fridolf, he dashed outside the door and locked it. And all of us stood outside and watched Fridolf through the window. He whimpered like a hungry little child, and one after another he quickly gobbled up the bread board and the water jug and fifteen plates. After that he started on the table; he broke off all four legs and ate so rapidly that the sawdust flew from his mouth, but he did say that, for asparagus, it was rather woody. He seemed to like the table top better, because he smacked his lips when he ate it, and said it was the best sandwich he'd had since he was a little boy. But by this time Daddy felt that Fridolf had recovered from his wasting disease, and he went in and told Fridolf that he'd have to try and manage without any more food for the two hours until dinner-time, and then he would get mashed turnips and boiled bacon. "Aye, aye, Cap'n," said Fridolf, wiping his mouth. "But just a moment, Cap'n," he added, and his eyes gleamed with eagerness, "when is supper-time and couldn't we have it a bit earlier?" '

Pippi put her head on one side, looked at Tommy and Annika, and then at their porridge plates.

'As I was saying, you certainly need a little sea voyage. That would soon cure your poor appetites.'

The postman was just passing the Settergreens' house on his way to Villekulla Cottage. He caught sight of Pippi through the window and shouted:

'Pippi Longstocking, there is a letter for you here!'

Pippi was so surprised that she nearly fell off the chair.

'A letter? For me? A real letter, I mean, a real letter? I shan't believe it until I see it.'

But it *was* a real letter—a letter with a lot of foreign stamps on the envelope.

'You read it, Tommy; you're good at that,' said Pippi.

'My dear Pippilotta,' Tommy read aloud. 'When you receive this, you might as well go down to the harbour and look for the *Hoppetossa*, because I am coming to take you to Canny Canny Island for a holiday. I think it's only right that you should see the country where your father has become such a mighty monarch. It's quite cosy here and I think you will like it. My faithful subjects are also very much looking forward to seeing the famous Princess Pippilotta. So there are no buts about it. You're coming—it is my royal and fatherly command.

A great big kiss and much love from your old father

KING EPHRAIM I, Longstocking,
Supreme Ruler over Canny Canny Island.'

When Tommy had finished reading the letter, you could have heard a pin drop in the kitchen.

6
Pippi Goes Aboard

One fine morning the *Hoppetossa* sailed into the harbour, decorated with flags and streamers from stem to stern. The members of the little town's brass band were standing on the quay, blowing a lively tune of welcome with all their might. Everyone in the little town had turned up to see Pippi meet her'father, King Ephraim I, Longstocking. A photographer was also ready to take a picture of their first meeting.

Pippi was so impatient that she was jumping

up and down, and no sooner had the gangway been lowered than Captain Longstocking and Pippi hurled themselves together with loud shrieks of joy. Captain Longstocking was so glad to see his daughter that he threw her several times up in the air. Pippi was just as excited, so she threw her father high in the air even more times. The only unhappy person was the photographer, because it was quite impossible for him to get a good picture when all the time either Pippi or her father were flying through the air.

Then Tommy and Annika came up to greet Captain Longstocking, but oh, how pale and miserable they looked! It was the first time they had come out after their illness.

Pippi had to go on board, of course, to see Fridolf and all her other friends among the seamen. Tommy and Annika were allowed to come with her. It was a new experience to walk about on a ship which had come from so far away, and Tommy and Annika were agog to see all there was to see. They looked specially eagerly for Agathon and Theodore, but Pippi said that they had left the ship long ago.

Pippi gave each of the sailors such a hug that they had difficulty in breathing for the next five' minutes. Then she picked up Captain Longstocking, put him on her shoulders, and carried him through the crowd and all the way home to Villekulla Cottage. Tommy and Annika walked behind hand in hand.

'Long live King Ephraim!' shouted everybody. They regarded this as a great day in the history of the town.

A few hours later, Captain Longstocking was in bed at Villekulla Cottage, asleep, and snoring so hard that the whole house trembled. Pippi, Tommy, and Annika were sitting at the table in the kitchen, where the remains of an excellent supper were still to be seen. Tommy and Annika sat quiet and thoughtful. What could they be thinking about? Well, Annika was thinking that, all things considered, she would rather be dead. And Tommy was trying to remember if there really was anything in the world that made life worth living, but there seemed to be nothing at all. Life was like a desert, he thought.

But Pippi was as happy as a lark. She stroked Mr Nelson, who was walking carefully, to and fro, between the plates on the table, she patted Tommy and Annika on the back, she whistled and sang, and now and then she danced a few steps and did not seem to notice that Tommy and Annika were so depressed.

'It'll be grand to go to sea again,' she said. 'Think of it—the sea—where you're free as a bird!'

Tommy and Annika sighed.

'I shall be jolly pleased to see Canny Canny Island, too. It'll be lovely to lie stretched out on the beach with my toes washed by the good old South Seas, and only have to open my mouth for a ripe banana to drop straight into it.'

Tommy and Annika sighed.

'And what fun to play with the little island children down there,' continued Pippi.

Tommy and Annika sighed.

'What are you sighing for?' asked Pippi. 'Don't you like sweet little island children?'

'Oh yes,' said Tommy. 'It's only that we keep on thinking what a long time it'll be before you come back to Villekulla Cottage.'

''Course,' said Pippi gaily. 'But that doesn't worry me at all. I think p'raps it'll be even more fun on Canny Canny Island.'

Annika turned a pale and despairing face towards Pippi.

'Oh, Pippi,' she said, 'how long d'you think you'll be away?'

'It's hard to say, really. Till around Christmas time, I should think.'

Annika gave a sob.

'Who knows?' said Pippi. 'P'raps it's so nice on Canny Canny Island that I shall want to stay there for ever. Hoppety-hop,' said Pippi and danced round again. 'A Cannibal Princess! That's not so dusty a job for one who's not been to school much.'

Tommy and Annika's eyes began to look strangely watery in their pale faces. Suddenly Annika flopped on the table and burst into tears.

'But come to think of it, I don't expect I shall want to stay there for ever,' said Pippi. 'You *can* have enough of court life and get sick of it all. So one fine day I expect I shall say: "Tommy and Annika! How about a trip home to Villekulla Cottage for a change?"'

'Oh, how lovely it'll be when you write and tell us you're coming,' said Tommy.

'Write!' said Pippi. 'Haven't you got ears in your heads? I'm not going to write. I'm just going to *say*: "Tommy and Annika, we're off home to Villekulla Cottage."'

Annika lifted her head from the table and Tommy said:

'What do you mean by that?'

'Mean?' said Pippi. 'Don't you understand plain English? Or could I really have forgotten to tell you that you're coming to Canny Canny Island? I felt quite sure that I'd told you.'

Tommy and Annika *leapt* from their chairs. They were breathing fast . . . But Tommy said:

'The things you say! Mummy and Daddy will never let us go.'

'Oh yes, they will,' said Pippi. 'I've already arranged it with your mother.'

There was complete silence in the kitchen of Villekulla Cottage for precisely five seconds. Then two loud shrieks were heard. They came from Tommy and Annika who hooted with joy.

Mr Nelson, who was sitting on the table trying to spread butter on his hat, looked up in surprise. His surprise was even greater when he saw Pippi, Tommy, and Annika join hands and start to dance round and round the room. They danced and shrieked so loudly that the ceiling lamp came loose and fell down to the floor. Mr Nelson threw the butter knife out of the window and he, too, started to dance.

'Is it really true?' asked Tommy when they had calmed down and crawled into the wood box to talk things over. Pippi nodded.

Yes! It was really true. Tommy and Annika were to go to Canny Canny Island. Of course, nearly all the ladies in the little town came to Mrs Settergreen and said:

'You *don't* mean to say that you're going to let your children go far away to the South Seas with *Pippi Longstocking*? You can't be serious!'

But Mrs Settergreen said:

'And why shouldn't I? The children have been ill, and they need a change of air; the doctor says so. All the time that I've known Pippi, she's never done anything which has been bad for Tommy and Annika. No one could be kinder to them than she is.'

'But, my dear! *Pippi Longstocking!* said the ladies disapprovingly.

'Exactly,' said Mrs Settergreen, 'Pippi Longstocking may not have very good manners, but she has a kind heart.'

And so it happened that, on a chilly evening in early spring, Tommy and Annika left the tiny little town for the first time in their lives to go out into the wide wide world together with Pippi. They were standing at the taffrail, all three of them, while the fresh evening breeze filled the sails of the Hoppetossa. Three of them? Well, there'were five, really, because the horse and Mr'Nelson were on deck, too.

All the children's school friends were standing on the quay and they were nearly in tears with sorrow and envy. Tomorrow they would have to go to school as usual. And they had been told to learn the names of all the islands in the South Seas for their geography homework. Tommy and Annika would have no homework to do for a long time. 'Health is more important than school work,' the doctor had said. 'And they'll have the South Sea Islands on the spot,' said Pippi.

Tommy and Annika's mother and father were also standing on the quayside, and Tommy and Annika felt a sudden tugging at their heart-strings when they saw their parents take out their handkerchiefs to wipe away a tear. But Tommy and Annika just could not help being happy all the same; they were so happy that it nearly hurt.

Slowly the *Hoppetossa* glided away from the quay.

'Tommy and Annika,' Mrs Settergreen called out, 'when you get to the North Sea, don't forget to put on *two* vests and . . .'

The rest of what she was about to say was drowned in the farewell shouts of the people on the quay, the wild neighing of the horse, Pippi's joyous shrieks, and Captain Longstocking's trumpeting when he blew his nose.

The voyage had begun. The *Hoppetossa* sailed away under the stars. Slabs of ice danced before the bow and the wind sang in the rigging.

'Oh, Pippi,' said Annika, 'I feel so excited. I think I want to be a pirate, too, when I'm grown up.'

7
Pippi Goes Ashore

'Land ho—Canny Canny Island straight ahead,' shouted Pippi one morning, when the dazzling rays of the sun were beating down out of a cloudless sky. She was standing by the look-out, dressed in nothing but a small piece of cloth tucked round her tummy.

They had sailed for days and nights, for weeks and months—over stormy oceans, and calm friendly seas; they had sailed by starlight and moonlight, under dark, threatening skies and in scorching sun. Yes, they had sailed for so long that Tommy and Annika had almost forgotten what it felt like to live at home in the little town.

Their mother would certainly have been surprised if she could have seen them as they were now. No more pale cheeks! Healthy and sunburnt and bright-eyed, they climbed about in the rigging, just like Pippi. The climate became warmer and warmer and they peeled off their garments, one by one, so that, in the end, the two children (who had crossed the North Sea so warmly clad, wearing two woollen vests) had turned into little brown berries without a stitch on except a cloth wound round their middles.

'Oh, we are lucky,' said Tommy and Annika every morning, when they woke up in the cabin which they shared with Pippi. Pippi was generally already up by then and steering the ship.

'A better sailor than my daughter never sailed the seven seas,' Captain Longstocking often said. He was quite right, too: Pippi could guide the *Hoppetossa* with a firm hand through the roughest breakers and past the most dangerous hidden rocks.

But now the voyage was over.

'Canny Canny Island straight ahead,' shouted Pippi.

And there it lay, covered with green palms and surrounded by the bluest of blue water.

Two hours later, the *Hoppetossa* ran into a little bay on the western side of the island. All the Canny Cannibals, men, women, and children, were waiting on the shore to receive their king and his red-haired daughter. The crowd surged forward when the gangway was lowered.

Shouts of 'Ussamkura, kussomkara,' were heard, which meant:

'Welcome back, fat white chief!'

King Ephraim, dressed in his blue corduroy suit, strode majestically down the gangway, as Fridolf, on the foredeck, played the new Canny Cannibal national anthem on a concertina: 'Here the conquering hero comes!'

King Ephraim raised his hand in greeting and shouted: 'Muoni manana!' which meant: 'Hallo, chums!'

Pippi walked behind him. She was carrying the horse! A murmur went through the crowd of Canny Cannibals. They had heard tales of Pippi and of her enormous strength, certainly, but it was quite a different matter to see it for themselves. Sedately Tommy and Annika walked ashore, too, and the whole of the crew followed, but at the time the Canny Cannibals had no eyes for anyone but Pippi. Captain Longstocking lifted her up and stood her on his shoulders, so that they could see her clearly, and once more a murmur passed through the crowd. But when, a moment later, Pippi herself lifted Captain Longstocking up on one of her shoulders and the horse on the other, the murmur rose to a roar, almost as loud as a hurricane.

The entire population of Canny Cannibal Island was no more than 126 people.

'It's just about the right number of subjects to have,' said King Ephraim. 'I couldn't keep track of them if I had more.'

They all lived in cosy little huts among the palm trees. The largest and finest one belonged to King Ephraim. The crew of the *Hoppetossa* had huts of their own, too, for living in when the *Hoppetossa* was anchored in the little bay, and where, as a matter of fact, she nearly always stayed nowadays. Only on rare occasions was it necessary to make an expedition to an island fifty miles to the north. You see, there was a shop there where they could buy snuff for Captain Longstocking.

A very pretty little hut had been newly built, specially for Pippi, underneath a coconut palm. There was ample room for Tommy and Annika in it, too. But before they could go into the hut to wash off the stains of travel, Captain Longstocking had something to show them. He grabbed Pippi's arm and led her down to the shore again.

'Here,' he said, pointing with a fat forefinger, 'here's the identical spot where I floated ashore that time when I was blown into the sea.'

The Canny Cannibals had raised a monument there to celebrate such a remarkable event. On the stone was the following inscription in Canny Cannibalish:

Across the great wide ocean came our fat white chief. This is the place where he floated ashore when the bread-fruit trees were in bloom. May he ever remain as fat and splendid as when he came.

Captain Longstocking read the inscription aloud to Pippi, Tommy, and Annika in a voice which trembled with emotion. Afterwards he blew his nose vigorously.

When the sun began to set and it was about to disappear into the vast bosom of the South Seas, the Canny Cannibals' drums called all the people to the royal square in the centre of the village where they held their feasts. There stood King Ephraim's splendid throne which was made of bamboo sticks and decorated with red hibiscus flowers. It was on this throne that he sat when he held his court. The Canny Cannibals had made a slightly smaller throne for Pippi, and had put it'beside her father's. They had even hastily constructed two small bamboo seats for Tommy and Annika as well.

The rolling of the drums grew louder and louder as King Ephraim, with great dignity, sat on his throne. He had shed his corduroy suit and was dressed in royal attire with a crown on his head, a straw skirt round his waist, a necklace of shark's teeth round his neck, and thick rings round his ankles. Pippi, quite unconcerned, perched herself on her throne. She was still wearing the same little cloth as before, but, to make herself look nice, she had stuck a few red and white flowers in her hair. So had Annika. But *not* Tommy—not for anything would he wear flowers in *his* hair.

King Ephraim had, of course, been away for a long time from his work of reigning, and now he began to reign for all he was worth. Meanwhile, the little Canny Cannibal children approached Pippi's throne. The nearer they came to Pippi and Tommy and Annika, the more awestruck they became. And besides, Pippi was a princess. When they had come close to Pippi they all, with one accord, knelt down and touched the ground with their foreheads.

Pippi quickly jumped down from the throne.

'Good gracious!' she said. 'If you're hunting the thimble I'd like to join in!'

She knelt down and moved her nose all over the ground.

'Somebody must have been here before us,' she said after a time. 'I'm definitely certain there isn't even a pin here.'

She sat on the throne once more. But no sooner had she done so than all the children again bent their heads to the ground in front of her.

'Have you lost something?' enquired Pippi. 'It isn't there anyway, because I've looked, so you might as well get up.'

Luckily, Captain Longstocking had been on the island for so long that some of the Canny Cannibals had learnt a little of his language. Of course, they did not know the meaning of difficult words like 'postal order' and 'Major-General', but they had picked up quite a lot just the same. Even the children knew some common expressions like 'don't touch' and so on. One small boy, called Momo, could speak the white people's language quite well, because he often stood near the huts of the crew, listening to their chatter. There was also a pretty little girl, called Moana, who knew almost as much.

Momo tried to explain to Pippi why they were kneeling before her.

'You be velly fine white princess,' he said.

'I not be velly fine white princess,' said Pippi in broken Canny Cannibalish. 'I be, on the whole, only Pippi Longstocking, and now be blowed to all this throning.'

She jumped down from the throne. So did King Ephraim, because he had finished his reigning business for the time being.

The sun sank like a red globe into the South Seas, and soon the sky was alight with stars. The Canny Cannibals lit an enormous camp fire in the royal square, and King Ephraim, Pippi, Tommy, Annika, and the crew of the *Hoppetossa* settled down on the grass to watch the Canny Cannibals dancing round the fire. The muffled rolling of the drums, the weird dance, the exotic scents from thousands of unseen flowers in the jungle, the stars twinkling in the sky above their heads—all these strange things filled Tommy and Annika with wonder, accompanied, as they were, by the unceasing sound of the restless waves of the ocean.

'I think it's a jolly good island,' said Tommy later, when Pippi, Annika, and he had snuggled into bed in their cosy little hut under the coconut palm.

'So do I,' said Annika. 'Don't you, Pippi?'

But Pippi lay quiet, with her feet on the pillow as she always did.

'Listen to the roar of the ocean,' she said dreamily.

8
Pippi Reproves a Shark

Very early next morning Pippi, Tommy, and Annika crawled out of their hut. But the Canny Cannibal children had already been awake for hours. Filled with excitement, they were sitting under the coconut palm, waiting for the white children to come out and play. They chattered sixteen to the dozen in Canny Cannibalish and their teeth flashed white in their black faces when they laughed.

Pippi led the whole crowd of children down to the shore. Tommy and Annika leapt for joy when they saw the fine white sand (where you could dig yourself in), and the very inviting blue sea. A coral reef, just off the island, served as a breakwater. Inside it, the water lay still and smooth as a mirror. All the children, the white ones and the black, threw off their clothes and rushed, shouting and laughing, into the water.

After the swim they rolled in the white sand, and Pippi and Tommy and Annika agreed that black skin was much the best because white sand on a black background looked so very funny. But, when Pippi had dug herself into the sand right up to her neck so that nothing but a freckled face and two red plaits were visible, that looked quite funny, too. All the children squatted round her for a chat.

'Tell about white children in white children's country,' said Momo to the freckled face.

'White children love pluttification,' said Pippi.

'It's multiplication,' said Annika. 'And besides,' she continued in an offended tone of voice, 'you can hardly say that we *love* it.'

'White children love pluttification,' persisted Pippi. 'White children go crackers if white children not have big doses pluttification every day.'

She was quite worn out with the effort of

speaking broken Canny Cannibalish and went on in her own language.

'If you come across a white child crying you can be pretty sure that the school has either gone up in flames, or that a half-term holiday has broken out, or that the teacher has forgotten to set homework for the children in pluttification. I hardly like to tell you what it's like when they're breaking up for their summer holidays. There's so much weeping and moaning it makes you wish you were dead when you hear it. There isn't a dry eye when the school door is shut for the summer. All the children walk home sobbing bitterly and they fairly hiccup with weeping when they think that it'll be several months before they have pluttification again. No misfortune can compare with it,' said Pippi, sighing heavily.

'What nonsense you do talk!' said Tommy and Annika.

Momo did not know the meaning of 'pluttification' and asked what it was. Tommy was on the point of explaining when Pippi forestalled him.

'Well, you see,' she said, 'it's like this: 7 times 7 is 102. Fun, isn't it?'

'It's not 102 at all,' said Annika.

'No—because 7 times 7 are 49,' said Tommy.

'Don't forget that we're on Canny Canny Island now,' said Pippi. 'The climate is quite different and it's much more fertile, so 7 times 7 are a lot more here than in other places.'

'Rubbish,' said Tommy and Annika.

The arithmetic lesson was interrupted by Captain Longstocking who came and told them that he and the whole crew and all the Canny Cannibals intended to sail to another island to'hunt wild boar for several days. Captain Longstocking was feeling in the mood for some fresh roast pork. The Canny Cannibal women were going with them to drive the boar out into the open with wild screams. This meant that the children would be left alone on Canny Canny Island.

'You don't mind, do you?' said Captain Longstocking.

'I give you three guesses,' said Pippi. 'The day that I hear of children minding being left to look after themselves without grown-ups, I'll learn all the pluttification tables backwards.'

'That's the spirit,' said Captain Longstocking.

And he, and all his subjects, armed with shields and spears, stepped into their big canoes and paddled away from Canny Canny Island.

Pippi put her hands round her mouth and shouted after them:

'Go in peace! But if you're not back in time for my fiftieth birthday I shall have an SOS sent out for you on the radio.'

When they found themselves alone, Pippi and Tommy and Annika and Momo and Moana and all the other children looked at each other delightedly. Now they had a lovely South Sea Island all to themselves for several days.

'What shall we do?' asked Tommy and Annika.

'First of all we're going to fetch our breakfast down from the trees,' said Pippi.

She herself quickly climbed up a palm tree for coconuts. Momo and the other Canny Cannibal children picked breadfruit and bananas. Pippi made up a fire on the beach and roasted the delicious breadfruit over it. The children sat down 'in a circle round her, and they all had a large' breakfast of breadfruit, coconut milk, and bananas.

There were no horses on Canny Canny Island, so all the island children were very taken with Pippi's horse. Those who were brave enough were allowed to have a ride on his back. Moana said she would like to go one day to the white people's country where they had such wonderful animals.

Mr Nelson was nowhere to be seen. He had

gone off on an expedition into the jungle, and there he had found some of his relations.

'What shall we do now?' said Tommy and Annika when they had all had enough of riding.

'White children want to see fine caves, yes, no?' asked Momo.

'White children certainly want to see fine caves, yes, *yes*,' said Pippi.

Canny Canny Island was a coral island. High coral cliffs fell steeply into the sea on the south side and there the sea waves had dug out the most splendid caves. Some of them were on the waterline and were filled by the sea, but there were others higher up in the cliff, and that was where the Canny Cannibal children used to play. They had stored up large quantities of coconuts and other good things to eat in the biggest cave. It was quite an adventure getting there. You had to work very carefully along the face of the cliff while hanging on to projecting stones and rocks. If you did not take care, you might easily fall into the sea. This would not, of course, have mattered much in the ordinary way, but in this particular place there were plenty of sharks that were very greedy to eat small children. In spite of this, the Canny Cannibal children used to amuse themselves by diving for pearl oysters; but then one of them always had to stand guard and shout,

'Shark! Shark!' the moment the fin of a shark appeared. Inside the big cave the Canny Cannibal children had a hoard of gleaming pearls which they had found in the oysters. They used the pearls for marbles, and they had no idea that those pearls were worth untold wealth in the lands of the white people. Captain Longstocking sometimes took a pearl or two with him when he went to buy snuff. In exchange, he brought back numerous things which he thought his subjects needed, but on the whole he felt that his faithful Canny Cannibals were better off as they were. And he had nothing against the children continuing to play marbles with the pearls.

Annika was horrified when Tommy told her to climb along the cliff to the big cave. The first part of the way was not very difficult. There was a fairly wide ledge to walk on, but it gradually became narrower and narrower, and for the last few yards to the cave you had to scramble and step wherever you could find a foothold.

'I can't,' gasped Annika. 'I can't!'

To move along a cliff where there was hardly anything to cling to, thirty feet above a sea full of sharks all waiting for you to fall down was not Annika's idea of having a good time.

Tommy got very angry.

'One should never bring sisters to the South Seas,' he said as he began to climb on the wall of rock. 'Just watch me! This is all you have to do—'

'Plop' was heard when Tommy tumbled into the water. Annika gave a loud shriek. Even the Canny Cannibal children were terrified. 'Shark! Shark!' they screamed, pointing at the sea. There was a fin showing in the water which was moving rapidly towards Tommy.

'Plop' was heard once more. It was Pippi jumping in. She reached Tommy about the same time as the shark. Tommy was screaming with fright. He felt the shark's pointed teeth scraping against his leg, but, at the very same moment, Pippi seized the bloodthirsty beast with both hands and held it up out of the water.

'What do you think you're doing?' she said. The shark looked round, surprised and uneasy; he could not breathe so well out of the water.

'Now promise not to do it any more and I'll let you go,' said Pippi severely. Then, with all her strength, she threw the shark far out to sea, and he wasted no time in swimming away from that place, and decided that, as soon as possible, he would go to the Atlantic instead.

Meanwhile, Tommy had climbed on to a little ledge where he sat trembling all over. His leg was bleeding. Pippi went to him. She behaved very oddly. First she lifted Tommy in the air and then she hugged him so hard that he nearly lost all his breath. Then she let go of him suddenly and sat down on the rock. She put her face in her hands and wept. Pippi wept! Tommy and Annika and all the Canny Cannibal children looked at her in surprise and alarm.

'You weep because Tommy nearly eaten,' suggested Momo.

'No,' said Pippi sulkily, wiping her eyes. 'I weep because poor little hungry shark not have any breakfast today.'

9
Pippi Reproves Jim
and Buck

The shark's teeth had only just grazed the skin on Tommy's leg, and when he had recovered from his fright he still wanted to go to the big cave. So Pippi made a rope of hibiscus fibre which she tied to a knob of rock. Then, nimble as a mountain goat, she nipped across to the cave where she fastened the other end of the rope. Even Annika was now brave enough to climb to the cave. With a stout rope to hang on to it was as easy as it could be.

It was a wonderful cave, so big that there was plenty of room for all the children.

'This cave is even better than our hollow oak tree at Villekulla Cottage,' said Tommy.

'No, not better, but just as good,' said Annika, who felt a heart-throb at the thought of the oak tree at home, and she would never admit that anything could be better than that.

Momo showed the three children the pile of coconuts and the cooked breadfruit which they had stored up in the cave. They could live there for weeks without starving. Moana brought and showed them a hollow bamboo cane full of the most splendid pearls and she gave Pippi and Tommy and Annika a handful each.

'Good place for marbles this, isn't it?' said Pippi.

It was simply beautiful to sit in the mouth of the cave and look out over the glittering sea. It was fun, too, to lie on one's tummy and see who could spit furthest out to sea. Momo was an expert at it, but was easily beaten by Pippi whom no one could equal.

'If it seems to be pouring with rain over in New Zealand today,' she said, 'it's my fault.'

Pippi shielded her eyes with her hand and looked out across the sea.

'I can see a ship over there,' she said. 'It's a very, very small steamer. I wonder what it's doing here.'

And she might well wonder. The steamer was approaching Canny Canny Island at a good speed. There were some sailors on board and also two white men, whose names were Jim and Buck. They were tough-looking, rough men, like real bandits. And that is exactly what they were.

Once, when Captain Longstocking had visited the shop to buy snuff, Jim and Buck were there, too. They saw Captain Longstocking put two unusually big and beautiful pearls on the counter, and they heard him say that on Canny Canny Island the children used pearls like these for marbles. Since that day, their one and only ambition had been to sail to Canny Canny Island to try and get hold of the pearls. They knew that Captain Longstocking was as strong as a giant, and they also had a great respect for the crew of the *Hoppetossa*, so they waited, and intended to act as soon as all the men folk went away hunting. Their chance had now come. Hidden behind a nearby island they watched through their binoculars until Captain Longstocking and all the sailors and Canny Cannibals had paddled away from Canny Canny Island. They waited just long enough for the canoes to get well out of sight.

'Let go the anchor,' shouted Buck when the ship had come close to the island. Pippi and all the children were watching them in silence from the cave above. The ship now lay at anchor. Jim and Buck jumped into a dinghy and rowed ashore. The sailors had been ordered to stay on board.

'We'll slip up to the village and take them by surprise,' said Jim. 'I expect only the women and children are at home.'

'Right-o,' said Buck. 'I saw so many women in the canoes, that I guess only the children are left on the island. I hope they're playing marbles! Ho-ho-ho!'

'Why?' shouted Pippi from the cave. 'Do you like playing marbles? I think leap-frog's just as much fun.'

Jim and Buck turned round in astonishment and caught sight of the heads of Pippi and all the children as they leant out of the cave. The men's faces broke into gratified smiles.

'Here they are,' said Jim.

'Good!' said Buck. 'We'll soon settle them.'

But they decided they had better use some cunning. After all, they did not know where the children kept their pearls, and the best plan would be to pretend to be friendly. They did not let it be known that they had come to Canny Canny Island to get pearls. No, indeed! 'We're out for a little pleasure trip,' they said. They were feeling hot and sticky, and Buck suggested they should have a swim, to begin with.

'I'll go back and fetch our swimming trunks,' he said.

He rowed away in the dinghy and Jim was left alone on the shore.

'Is this a good place for bathing?' he shouted to the children in a wheedling voice.

'Couldn't be better,' said Pippi. 'Couldn't be better for sharks. They bathe here every day.'

'Nonsense,' said Jim, 'I can't see a single shark.'

But he felt rather worried all the same, and when Buck returned with the trunks he repeated what Pippi had said.

'What rot,' said Buck. Then he shouted to Pippi: 'Was it you who said it's dangerous to bathe here?'

'No,' replied Pippi. 'I never said it was.'

'That's queer,' said Jim. 'Didn't you tell me there were sharks here?'

'Yes, I did . . . but dangerous? No, hardly that. My own grandfather bathed here last year.'

'Well, that's all right, then,' said Buck.

'And Grandfather came home from hospital only last Friday,' continued Pippi, 'with the smartest wooden legs an old man ever wore.'

She spat thoughtfully into the water.

'So you can hardly say it's dangerous. But you can expect to part with the odd arm or leg if you want to bathe here. Wooden legs cost only a shilling a pair, and I don't think you need feel you have to go without a health-giving swim just for the sake of economy.'

She spat once more.

'Grandfather takes quite a childish delight in his wooden legs. He says he doesn't know how he could manage without them when he's in for a fight.'

'Do you know what I think?' said Buck. 'I think you're lying. Your grandfather must be an old man. He surely wouldn't want to fight.'

'Wouldn't he just,' shouted Pippi, shrilly. 'He's the fiercest old man that ever banged his enemy on the head with a wooden leg. If he's not allowed to fight from morning till night he doesn't know what to do with himself and bites his own nose with rage.'

'What nonsense!' said Buck. 'How could he bite his own nose?'

'He can,' Pippi assured him. 'He climbs up on a chair to do it.'

Buck wrestled with the problem for a moment, then he swore and growled:

'I'm sick of listening to your absurd stories. Come on, Jim, let's get undressed.'

'Another thing,' said Pippi, 'is that Grandfather has the world's longest nose. He has five parrots, and all five of them can sit, one beside the other, on his nose.'

At this Buck became really angry.

'Let me tell you something, you red-headed little brat! You're certainly the biggest liar I ever met. You ought to be ashamed of yourself. Do you really expect me to believe that five parrots can sit in a row on your grandfather's nose? Own up that you're lying.'

'Yes,' said Pippi sadly. 'It is a lie.'

'There you are!' said Buck. 'Just what I said.'

'It's a terrible, wicked lie,' said Pippi more sadly still.

'I knew it all the time,' said Buck.

''Cos the fifth parrot,' shouted Pippi, bursting into a flood of tears, 'the fifth parrot *has to stand on one leg.*'

'Go to blazes,' said Buck, and he and Jim went behind a bush to undress.

'But, Pippi, you haven't got a grandfather,' said Annika reproachfully.

'No,' Pippi replied in a cheerful tone of voice. 'Are they compulsory?'

Buck was the first to appear in swimming trunks. He dived skilfully from a rock and swam out to sea. The children watched him intently from the cave. Suddenly, they saw the fin of a shark flash above the water.

'Shark! Shark!' shouted Momo.

Buck, who was enjoying himself greatly and was treading water, turned his head and caught sight of the fearful, hungry fish coming straight towards him.

No one could ever have swum faster than Buck did then. In two frantic seconds he reached dry land and rushed out of the water. He was frightened and angry, and he evidently blamed Pippi for the sharks in the water.

'You ought to be ashamed of yourself,' he shouted. 'The sea is *full* of sharks.'

'That's just what I told you,' said Pippi, smugly. 'I don't always tell lies, you see.'

Jim and Buck retired behind the bush to put their clothes on again. They felt that now was the time to begin to think about the pearls. Nobody knew how long Captain Longstocking and the others would be away.

'Listen, my dears,' said Buck, 'I've been told there's supposed to be good pearl fishing in these parts. Is it true, d'you know?'

'I should jolly well say there is,' said Pippi. 'The pearl oysters fairly rattle round your feet wherever you walk on the bottom of the sea. Just you go down and try for yourself.'

But Buck had no wish to do so.

'There are large pearls in every oyster,' said Pippi. 'Like this one.'

She held up a huge, gleaming pearl.

Jim and Buck were so excited that they could hardly restrain themselves.

'Have you got any more of those?' asked Jim. 'We'd like to buy them from you.'

This was not true, because Jim and Buck had no money for pearls. It was just a trick by which they hoped to steal them.

'Well, I should say we've got at least eight or nine pints of pearls in the cave,' said Pippi.

Jim and Buck could not hide their pleasure.

'Good,' said Buck. 'Just bring 'em here and we'll buy the lot.'

'Oh no, you won't,' said Pippi. 'What d'you think the poor children would play marbles with then?'

There was much discussion before Jim and Buck realized that they could not obtain the pearls by trickery. But what they could not have by cunning they would take by force. And now they knew where the pearls were. All they had to do was to climb up to the cave and seize them.

Climb up to the cave? Yes! While the discussion went on, Pippi, just to make sure, had untied the hibiscus rope. It was now lying safely inside the cave.

Jim and Buck were far from eager to try and climb across to the cave. But there did not seem to be anything else they could do.

'Go on,' said Buck.

'No-o, you go, Buck,' said Jim.

'YOU *go*, *Jim*,' said Buck. He was the stronger of the two. So Jim began to climb. Desperately he grabbed hold of any projections he could reach, while cold sweat ran down his back.

'Mind you hang on and don't fall in,' said Pippi encouragingly.

And then Jim fell into the sea. Buck, on the beach, shouted and swore. Jim shouted, too, because he saw two sharks making straight for him. When they were not more than a yard away, Pippi threw down a coconut right in front of their noses. This frightened them away long enough for Jim to reach the shore and climb up to the little ledge. His clothes were dripping with water and he looked a miserable sight. Buck cursed him.

'If you think it's so easy, go and do it yourself,' said Jim.

'All right,' said Buck, '*I'll* show you how it's done,' and he began to climb.

All the children peeped out at him. Annika felt rather frightened when he came nearer and nearer.

'Hi! Don't step there, you'll fall in,' said Pippi.

'Where?' said Buck.

'There,' said Pippi, pointing at his feet. Buck looked down . . .

'It's a dreadful waste of coconuts,' said Pippi a second later as she threw one into the sea to stop the sharks eating up Buck, who was wriggling unhappily in the water. But up he came again, angry as a bull, for he was not one to be easily frightened. He immediately started on another climb, because he was determined to reach the cave and get hold of the pearls.

This time he found it easier. When he had nearly reached the mouth of the cave he shouted triumphantly:

'Now I'll make you pay for everything.'

Then Pippi put out a finger and poked him in the stomach.

Splash!

'I wish you'd taken the coconut with you when you dropped off,' shouted Pippi after him, hitting an inquisitive shark on the nose. But other sharks came, and she had to throw more coconuts. One of them happened to fall on Buck's head.

'Oh *dear*, was that you?' said Pippi when Buck yelled with pain. 'From here you look exactly like a horrid big shark.'

Jim and Buck now decided to wait until the children left the cave.

'Sooner or later hunger will bring them out of there,' said Buck grimly. 'And then they'll be sorry.'

He shouted to the children:

'It seems a pity that you'll have to sit in that cave until you starve to death.'

'Very kind of you,' said Pippi. 'But you needn't worry about us for the next fortnight or so. Perhaps after that, we may have to start to ration the coconuts a little.'

She cracked a large coconut, drank the milk, and ate some of the delicious kernel.

Jim and Buck cursed loudly. The sun was beginning to set, and they prepared to spend the night on the beach. They dared not row out to the steamer to sleep there, because that would have given the children the chance to run off with all the pearls. They lay down on the hard rock in their wet clothes. It was very uncomfortable.

Inside the cave sat all the children, their eyes twinkling, and they feasted on coconuts and breadfruit. It tasted very good, and everybody was excited and happy. Every now and then they popped their heads out to look at Jim and Buck. Because of the gathering darkness they could hardly see the two bandits on the ledge of rock, but they could hear swearing down below.

Suddenly the rain started pelting down, the violent kind of rain which you get in the tropics. A solid sheet of water poured from the sky. Pippi put the merest tip of her nose outside the cave.

'I must say, some people are lucky,' she shouted to Jim and Buck.

'Just what do you mean?' asked Buck hopefully. He thought that perhaps the children had now changed their minds and would let them have the pearls. 'What do you mean by some people being lucky?'

'I was just thinking how jolly lucky you were to be soaked already before this *torrent* of rain started. Otherwise the rain would have made you wet through, wouldn't it?'

There was swearing below on the ledge, but you could not tell whether it came from Jim or Buck.

'Good night to you both, and sweet dreams,' said Pippi. 'That's what we're going to have, anyway.'

The children all lay down on the floor of the cave. Tommy and Annika nestled at Pippi's side with her hands in theirs. They were warm and cosy in the cave, and they could hear the rushing sound of the rain outside.

10
Pippi Gets Tired of Jim and Buck

The children slept soundly all night—but not so Jim and Buck. They kept on swearing at the rain, and when it stopped, they began quarrelling for a change. Jim blamed Buck, and Buck blamed Jim for not seizing the pearls, and whose stupid idea was it, anyway, to come to Canny Canny Island? But when the sun rose and dried their wet clothes and they saw Pippi's bright face in the entrance to the cave and heard her cheery 'Good morning,' they were more determined than ever to seize the pearls and leave the island as rich men. The trouble was that they could not think how they were going to do it.

Pippi's horse had started to wonder what had become of Pippi, Tommy, and Annika. Mr Nelson had returned from the meeting with his kinsfolk in the jungle, and he, too, was puzzled; and he was worried about what Pippi would say when she discovered that he had lost his little straw hat.

The horse, with Mr Nelson, who had jumped up on to his hindquarters, trotted off to look for Pippi. After some time he reached the southern side of the island . . . Then he saw Pippi's head pop out of a cave. He neighed happily.

'Look, Pippi! There's your horse!' shouted Tommy.

'And Mr Nelson is sitting on his back!' shouted Annika.

Jim and Buck overheard the children talking. They learned that the horse, trotting along the shore, belonged to Pippi, that red-headed nuisance in the cave above them.

Buck went up to the horse and grabbed his mane.

'Listen, you little devil,' he shouted. 'I'm going to kill your horse.'

'Oh, surely you wouldn't kill my lovely horse,' said Pippi, 'my dear kind little horse. You can't mean it.'

'Looks as if I should have to,' said Buck. 'That is, if you don't bring us the pearls. All of them, mind you! If you don't I'll kill the horse this very instant.'

Pippi looked at him seriously.

'Please,' she said. 'Oh, please don't kill my horse, and please let the children keep their pearls.'

'You heard what I said,' retorted Buck. 'Bring the pearls at once! Or else . . .'

Then he whispered to Jim:

'I'll teach her! When she brings the pearls, I'll beat her black and blue to pay her out for last night. We'll take the horse with us and sell it on some other island.'

He shouted to Pippi:

'Well, what about it? Are you coming, or not?'

'I might as well,' said Pippi. 'But don't forget, it was your idea.'

She leapt nimbly from one small ledge to another as easily as if there had been the smoothest path, and then down to the level place where Buck, Jim, and the horse were standing. She stopped in front of Buck and stood there, small and slight, with the little cloth round her tummy and the two red plaits sticking straight out. Her eyes had a dangerous glint in them.

'Where are the pearls?' Buck shouted.

'There aren't going to be any pearls today,' said Pippi. 'There's going to be leap-frog instead.'

When Buck heard this, he roared so fiercely that Annika trembled with fright as she stood listening in the cave above.

'This is the limit. Now I'm going to kill both you and the horse,' he yelled, and charged at Pippi.

'Steady on, my good man,' said Pippi. Grasping him round the waist, she threw him three yards into the air, and he landed with a bump on the rock. Then Jim went into action. He aimed a terrible blow at Pippi, but she jumped to one side with a confident smile, and a second later Jim, also, was sailing skywards. Jim and Buck sat side by side on the rock, groaning loudly. Pippi went up to them and gripped them both by the scruffs of their necks.

'You're *much* too fond of playing marbles,' she said. 'It's high time you did some work and stopped thinking of nothing but fun and games.'

She carried them to the dinghy and threw them in.

'Off you go, home to your mother, and ask her if you can have twopence to buy stone marbles with,' she said. 'They're just as good as pearls.'

Very soon, their ship steamed away from Canny Canny Island, never to be seen again in those waters.

Pippi patted her horse. Mr Nelson jumped up on her shoulder. And from behind the furthest point of the island a long line of canoes appeared. Captain Longstocking and his company were joyfully returning home from their hunting. Pippi shouted and waved to them, and they waved back with their paddles.

Pippi quickly secured the rope again, so that Tommy, Annika, and the others could leave the cave in safety. And when, a little later, the canoes anchored in the little bay beside the *Hoppetossa*, the whole crowd of children were already there on the shore to welcome them.

Captain Longstocking patted Pippi.

'And how have you fared while I've been away?' he asked.

'Oh, fine,' said Pippi.

'But, Pippi, we haven't,' said Annika. 'Lots of awful things nearly happened.'

'Oh yes, of course, I forgot,' said Pippi. 'We haven't been getting along fine at all, Daddy. The moment you turn your back things begin to happen.'

'My dear child, what's been happening?' exclaimed Captain Longstocking anxiously.

'Something awful,' said Pippi. 'Mr Nelson lost his straw hat.'

11
Pippi Leaves Canny Canny Island

Happy days followed, happy days in a warm, enchanted world, full of sunshine and glittering blue water and sweet-smelling flowers.

Tommy and Annika were by this time so brown that you could hardly tell the difference between them and the Canny Cannibal children. And there was not the tiniest bit of Pippi's face which did not have a freckle on it.

'This trip is a real beauty treatment for me,'

she said contentedly. 'I'm frecklier and more beautiful than ever now. If I go on like this I shall soon be quite irresistible.'

But Momo and Moana and all the other Canny'Cannibal children thought Pippi irresistible already. They had never had such a good time in their lives before, and they were just as fond of Pippi as Tommy and Annika were. Of course, they liked Tommy and Annika, too, and Tommy and Annika liked them back. So they all had a wonderful time together, playing from morning till night. They were often in the cave. Pippi had put some blankets there, and when they wanted to do so, they could sleep in the cave, even more comfortably than on that first night. She had also made a rope ladder which led to the water below the cave, and all the children climbed up and down it, bathed and splashed to their heart's content. Yes, it was quite safe to bathe there now. Pippi had fenced in a large area with a net, so that the sharks could not get near them. It was great fun to swim in and out of the caves which had water in them. Even Tommy and Annika had learnt how to dive for oysters. The first pearl that Annika found was a large beautiful pinky one. She made up her mind to take it home and have it set in a ring as a souvenir of Canny Canny Island.

Sometimes they pretended that Pippi was

Buck, trying to make his way to the cave to steal pearls. Then Tommy would pull up the rope ladder and Pippi had to climb up the face of the cliff the best way she could. All the children shouted, 'Buck's coming, Buck's coming,' when she put her head into the cave. Then, one after another, they were allowed to poke her in the tummy so that she toppled over backwards down into the sea. There she splashed about with only her feet showing out of the water, and the children laughed so much that they nearly fell out of the cave.

When they tired of the cave, they could go to their bamboo house. Pippi and the children had shared in the building of it, but Pippi had done most of the work. It was large and square, and was made of slender bamboo canes. You could climb in it and on it just as you liked. A tall coconut palm was growing close to the house. Pippi had chopped steps in the trunk of the palm tree so that you could go right up to the top and see a fine view from there. Between two other palm trees Pippi had fixed a swing, made of hibiscus rope. It was an extra specially good one. If you swung really high, and then threw yourself at top speed out of the swing, you landed in the water. Pippi swung so enormously high that she flew far out to sea. 'One fine day I expect I'll land in Australia, and it won't be much fun for the person whose head I drop on to,' she said.

The children sometimes made trips into the jungle to a place where there was a high mountain and a waterfall which tumbled down a steep part of it. Pippi had made up her mind to ride down the waterfall in a barrel, and sure enough she did. She brought one of the barrels from the *Hoppetossa*, and got into it. Momo and Tommy put the lid on and gave the barrel a push towards the waterfall. It hurtled down the fall at a colossal speed and was finally smashed to pieces. All the children saw Pippi disappear in the swirling torrent, and they thought they would never see her again. But before long she bobbed up to the surface, came out of the water, and said:

'These water-butts go a pretty good pace, I must say.'

The days went by, and the rainy season was about to begin, when Captain Longstocking would shut himself in his hut and contemplate. He was afraid Pippi would find it dull during the rains on Canny Canny Island. Tommy and Annika thought more and more often about their mother and father, and wondered how they were getting on. They were also very eager to be home for Christmas, so they were not so disappointed as one might think when Pippi said, one morning:

'Tommy and Annika, what about spending some time at Villekulla Cottage for a change?'

It was a sad day for Momo and Moana and the other Canny Cannibal children when Pippi, Tommy, and Annika went on board the *Hoppetossa*. But Pippi promised that they would come back to Canny Canny Island very, very often. The Canny Cannibal children had made garlands of white flowers which they hung round Pippi, Tommy, and Annika's necks as a parting gift. While the ship sailed away, a sad song of farewell was heard coming across the water. Captain Longstocking was also standing on the shore. He had to stay behind to rule his subjects. It was Fridolf who had taken on the duty of seeing the children home. Captain Longstocking blew his nose a number of times in a handkerchief smelling of snuff as he waved goodbye. Tears gushed out of Pippi, Tommy, and Annika's eyes'and they waved and waved to Captain Longstocking and the children until they could see them no longer.

A fair wind carried them on their way.

'We'd better bring out your woolly vests in good time before we reach the North Sea,' said Pippi.

'Oh! What a bore,' said Tommy and Annika.

It was soon evident that the *Hoppetossa*, in spite

of the fair wind, could not possibly reach home in time for Christmas. Tommy and Annika were very disappointed when they were told. Think of it! No Christmas tree and no presents!

'We might just as well have stayed on Canny Canny Island,' said Tommy, huffily.

Annika thought of her mother and father, and felt that she would be glad to get home in any case, but it was certainly disappointing to miss Christmas. Tommy and Annika were agreed about that all right.

One dark evening at the beginning of January, Pippi, Tommy, and Annika caught sight of the welcoming light of the little town. They were home at last.

'Well, here's the end of *that* South Sea trip,' said Pippi, as she walked down the gangway with the horse.

No one was on the quay to meet them, for nobody knew when they would arrive. Pippi lifted Tommy, Annika, and Mr Nelson on to the horse, and off they went to Villekulla Cottage. The horse had to lift his legs high, because the streets and the roads were deep in snow. Tommy and Annika could hardly see through the whirling snow. Soon they would be with their mother and father. And suddenly they felt they could not wait any longer.

There was a light shining from the Settergreens' house, and through the window Tommy and Annika could see their mother and father sitting by the dining-table.

'There's Mummy and Daddy,' said Tommy, sounding very pleased.

But Villekulla Cottage was in complete darkness and was covered in snow.

Annika could not bear the thought of Pippi going in there all alone.

'Please, Pippi, stay with us the first night,' she said.

'No, but many thanks all the same,' said Pippi, and stepped deep into the snow outside the gate. 'I've got to get things organized at Villekulla Cottage.'

She plunged on through the deep snow-drifts into which she sank right up to her waist. The horse followed.

'But it'll be so cold,' Tommy protested, 'there hasn't been a fire in the cottage for ever so long.'

'Nonsense,' said Pippi. 'So long as the heart's warm and ticks properly, you don't feel the cold.'

12
Pippi Longstocking Does not Want to Grow Up

Oh, how Tommy and Annika's mother and father hugged and kissed their children! Then they gave them a good supper and tucked them up in bed. They sat for a long time by the children's beds, listening to the tales of all the exciting things which had happened on Canny Canny Island. They were all very happy to be together again. There was only one fly in the ointment—they had not been at home for Christmas. Tommy and Annika did not want their mother to know how disappointed they were to have missed the Christmas tree and the presents, but they were sad about it all the same. It always takes a little time to settle down when you have been away and it would have helped enormously to have come back on Christmas Eve.

Tommy and Annika also felt a little sorry when they thought of Pippi. By now she would be in bed at Villekulla Cottage with her feet on the pillow, and there would be no one there to tuck her up. They decided to go and see her as early as they could on the following day.

But, on the following day, their mother did not want to part with them as she had not seen them for such a long time. Besides, their grandmother was coming to dinner, specially to see the children now they had come home. Tommy and Annika wondered anxiously what Pippi could be doing all day by herself, and when it began to get dark they could not bear it any longer.

'Please, Mummy, we *must* go and see Pippi,' said Tommy.

'Off you go, then,' said Mrs Settergreen. 'But don't stay long.'

Tommy and Annika scampered off.

When they reached the garden gate of Villekulla Cottage they stopped short and could hardly believe their eyes. The picture they saw was just like a Christmas card. The whole house was covered in soft snow and there were cheerful lights shining from every window. The flame of a burning torch outside the front door threw flickering beams across the gleaming snow. The path had been cleared, so Tommy and Annika could now walk up to the porch without sinking into drifts of snow.

They were just stamping the snow off their boots in the porch when the door opened, and there stood Pippi.

'A happy Christmas to you in this cottage,' she said. Then she pushed them into the kitchen. Heavens! If there wasn't a Christmas tree! The candles were lit, and seventeen sparklers, hooked on to the Christmas tree, were burning and spluttering and giving out a lovely smell. The table was laden with every kind of Christmas food: a large ham, coated in breadcrumbs, and decorated with fringes of tissue-paper, home-made sausages, and Christmas pudding. Pippi had even made ginger biscuits, in the shapes of boys and girls, and saffron bread. A roaring fire burned in the kitchen range, and close to the wood box stood the horse, pawing the floor delicately with his foot. Mr Nelson was jumping about in the tree in between the sparklers.

'He's supposed to be the Christmas angel,' said Pippi, severely, 'but do you think I can get him to sit still at the top?'

Tommy and Annika were speechless.

'Oh, Pippi,' said Annika at last, 'how beautiful! But how did you manage to do it all in the time?'

'I have an industrious disposition,' said Pippi.

Tommy and Annika were filled with sudden joy and happiness.

'I *am* glad we're home at Villekulla Cottage again,' said Tommy.

They sat down at the table and ate their fill of ham, sausages, pudding, ginger biscuits, and saffron bread, and they thought the feast tasted even better than bananas and breadfruit.

'But, Pippi! It isn't Christmas time,' said Tommy.

'Yes, it is,' said Pippi. 'Villekulla Cottage's calendar has lost a lot of time. I shall have to take it to a calendar repairer and have it seen to, so that it catches up again.'

'*What* a good thing!' said Annika. 'So we didn't miss our Christmas, after all—though, of course, we didn't get any presents.'

'Ah, I was thinking the very same thing,' said Pippi. 'I've hidden your presents. You'll have to look for them.'

Tommy and Annika went red in the face with excitement. Before you could wink twice they got up from the table and started hunting. In the wood box Tommy found a large parcel; on it was written 'TOMMY'. It contained a splendid paint-box. Underneath the table Annika found a parcel with her name on it, and inside the parcel was a pretty red sunshade.

'I shall take it with me next time we go to Canny Canny Island,' said Annika.

Inside the chimney corner hung two parcels. One contained a toy jeep for Tommy, and the other, a doll's tea-service for Annika. A little parcel was hanging from the horse's tail and in it was a clock for the mantelpiece of Tommy and Annika's nursery.

When they had found all their presents they both gave Pippi a big hug. She was standing by the kitchen window, looking at the quantities of snow in the garden.

'Tomorrow, we're going to build a big igloo,' she said. 'And we'll have a candle burning in it in the evenings.'

'Oh yes, let's,' said Annika, feeling more and more pleased to be home again.

'And let's make a ski-slope running down from the roof and into the snow below,' said Pippi. 'I want to teach the horse to ski, but I'm blowed if I know whether he will need four skis, or only two.'

'Hurray! We're going to have a lovely time tomorrow,' said Tommy. 'Wasn't it lucky we came in the middle of the Christmas hols?'

'We shall always have a lovely time here at Villekulla Cottage and on Canny Canny Island and everywhere,' said Annika.

Pippi nodded in agreement. All three were now sitting on the kitchen table. A shadow suddenly passed across Tommy's face.

'I never want to grow up,' he said firmly.

'Nor me,' said Annika.

'No, that's nothing to pine for,' said Pippi. 'Grown-ups never have any fun. All they have is a lot of dull work and stupid clothes and corns and nincum tax.'

'It's called income tax,' said Annika.

'It's all the same rubbish,' said Pippi. 'And they're full of superstition and silly ideas. They think it's bad luck to put a knife in your mouth when you eat, and things like that.'

'And they don't know how to play,' said Annika. 'Ugh! Fancy having to grow up!'

'And who said we have to?' asked Pippi. 'If I remember rightly, I've got some pills somewhere.'

'What kind of pills?' said Tommy.

'Awfully good pills for those who don't want to grow up,' said Pippi, jumping down from the table. She searched in all the cupboards and drawers, and after a short time she brought out what looked exactly like three yellow dried peas.

'Peas!' said Tommy in surprise.

'That's what *you* think,' said Pippi. 'It isn't peas. It's squigglypills. An old Red Indian Chief gave them to me a long time ago in Rio when I happened to mention that I didn't care very much for growing up.'

'Is that all you have to do—just take those little pills?' asked Annika doubtfully.

'Yes,' Pippi assured her. 'But you must eat them in the dark and say:

'Little squiggle, you are clever,
I do not want to *grew* up ever.'

'You mean "grow", don't you?' said Tommy.

'I said "grew", and I mean "grew",' said Pippi. 'That's the whole secret, you see. Most people say "grow" and that's the worst thing you can do, because it makes you grow more than ever. Once there was a boy who ate pills like these. He said "grow" instead of "grew" and he began to grow so much it was frightening. Lots and lots of yards every day. It was tragic. Mind you, it was all very well so long as he could walk

107

about and graze straight out of big apple trees, rather like a giraffe. But it wasn't long before he got too tall for that. When his aunts came on a visit and they wanted to say: "What a fine big fellow you've grown into", they had to shout to him through a megaphone. All you could see of him was his long thin legs, like two flagpoles, which disappeared in the clouds. We never heard a sound from him again except once, when he took it into his head to lick the sun and got a blister on his tongue. Then he yelled so loudly that the flowers down on Earth all wilted. That was the very last sign of life we ever had from him. But I suppose his legs are still walking about in Rio and causing a lot of disturbance in the traffic, if I'm not much mistaken.'

'I daren't take a pill,' said Annika, frightened, 'in case I say the wrong thing.'

'You won't,' said Pippi, consolingly. 'If I thought you'd do that, I wouldn't let you have one, because it would be so dull to have only your legs to play with. Tommy and me and your legs—that would be a queer sight!'

'Don't be silly, Annika,' said Tommy. 'Of course you won't say it wrong.'

They blew out all the candles on the Christmas tree. The kitchen was quite dark except near the stove, where you could see the fire glowing behind the bars. The children sat down silently in a circle in the middle of the floor. They held hands. Pippi gave Tommy and Annika a squigglypill each. They could feel the excitement creeping up and down their spines. Imagine it— in a moment or two they would have swallowed the strange pills and then they would never, never have to grow up. Wasn't it wonderful?

'Now!' whispered Pippi.

They swallowed their pills, saying, all three together:

> 'Little squiggle, you are clever,
> I do not want to grew up ever.'

It was all over. Pippi lit the lamp.

'Good!' she said. 'Now we shan't have to grow up and have corns and other miseries. Of course, the pills have been in my cupboard for so long that I can't be *quite* sure they haven't lost their goodness. But we must hope for the best.'

Something had just occurred to Annika.

'But, Pippi!' she cried in dismay, 'you were going to be a pirate when you grew up!'

'Oh, I can be a pirate anyway,' said Pippi. 'I can be a teeny-weeny ferocious pirate, spreading death and destruction, all the same.'

She looked thoughtful.

'Supposing,' she said, 'supposing that after many, many years have gone by, a lady comes walking past here one day and sees us running in the garden and playing. Perhaps she will ask you, Tommy, "And how old are you, my little friend?" And you say: "Fifty-three, if I'm not mistaken." '

Tommy laughed heartily.

'I shall be rather small for my age, I think,' he said.

'Yes,' admitted Pippi, 'but you can always say that you were bigger when you were smaller.'

Tommy and Annika now remembered that their mother had told them not to stay long.

'I'm afraid we've got to go home,' said Tommy.

'But we'll be back tomorrow,' said Annika.

'Good,' said Pippi. 'We're starting on the igloo at eight o'clock.'

She saw them off at the gate and her red plaits bobbed round her head as she ran back to Villekulla Cottage.

'Well!' said Tommy a little later when he was brushing his teeth. 'If I hadn't known they were squigglypills I could have sworn they were just ordinary peas.'

Annika was standing by the nursery window in her pink pyjamas, looking towards Villekulla Cottage.

'Look! I can see Pippi!' she shouted in delight.

Tommy rushed to the window. Yes! So could he! Now that the trees were bare you could see right into Pippi's kitchen.

Pippi was sitting by the table, leaning her head on her arms. She was gazing dreamily at the flickering light of a small candle in front of her.

'She's . . . she's looking so lonely, somehow,' said Annika; and her voice trembled a little. 'Oh, Tommy, I wish it was morning and we could go to her straight away.'

They stood there, silently looking out into the winter night. The stars were shining above the roof of Villekulla Cottage and Pippi was inside. She would always be there. It was wonderful to remember that. The years would pass, but Pippi and Tommy and Annika would never grow up. That is, if the squigglypills were still good! Spring and summer would come, and then autumn and winter, again and again, but their games would continue. Tomorrow they would build an igloo and make a ski-run from the roof of Villekulla Cottage. In the spring they would climb in the hollow oak tree where ginger-beer grew. They would hunt the thimble, they would sit in the wood box and tell stories. They would, perhaps, go to Canny Canny Island sometimes, and see Momo and Moana and the others. But they would always come back to Villekulla Cottage. Yes! It was a very comforting thought—Pippi would always, always be there.

'If only she'd look this way we could wave to her,' said Tommy.

But Pippi only gazed in front of her with dreamy eyes.

Then she blew out the candle.

About the author

Astrid Lindgren was born in Vimmerby, Sweden in 1907. She married Sture Lindgren in 1931 and had a son and a daughter. Pippi Longstocking was created when Astrid made up a story about an extremely strong, red-haired girl for her daughter who was ill with pneumonia.

The first Pippi Longstocking book was published in Sweden in 1945 and was an instant hit with children, although some adults feared that Pippi was a bit too independent and perhaps unsuitable for girls to read. In the end though everyone agreed that Pippi was a wonderful and endearing character and her stories have since been published all over the world, including the English translation published in 1954.

Astrid Lindgren wrote over 40 books for children and broadcast widely on TV and radio—reading her stories.

In 1989 a theme park dedicated to the author—Astrid Lindgren Varld—was opened in her home town of Vimmerby.

Astrid Lindgren was the recipient of many major awards for her writing, including the prestigious Hans Christian Andersen Award and The International Book Award. She died in 2002 at the age of 94.

Other books by Astrid Lindgren

Pippi is nine years old. She lives alone in her own
house with a horse and a monkey, and she does
exactly as she pleases. She has no mother and she believes
her father is the king of a cannibal island. She has never
learnt to look after herself and has never been to school.
Her friends, Tommy and Annika, are green with envy—but
although they have to go to school and go to bed
when they are told, they still have time to join
Pippi on all her great adventures.

ISBN-13: 978-0-19-275413-4
ISBN-10: 0-19-275413-0

Whenever Tommy and Annika are with
Pippi Longstocking, they have the most wonderful
adventures. But the most thrilling time by far is
when Pippi's father, a cannibal king, comes to visit.
Pippi is soon making plans to sail away with him,
back to his island. Tommy and Annika can't bear to see
her leave—life without Pippi will be very dull indeed...

ISBN-13: 978-0-19-275482-0
ISBN-10: 0-19-275482-3

Other Oxford Fiction

How to Survive Summer Camp

Jacqueline Wilson

ISBN-13: 978-0-19-275019-8
ISBN-10: 0-19-275019-4

Typical! Mum and Uncle Bill have gone off on a swanky honeymoon, while Stella's been dumped at Evergreen Summer Camp. Guess what? She's not happy about it!

Things get worse. Stella loses all her hair (by accident!), has to share a dorm with snobby Karen and Louise, and is forced into terrifying swimming lessons with Uncle Pong! It looks as if she's in for a nightmare summer—how can Stella possibly survive?

A hilarious summer story from the award-winning author of *Double Act, Bad Girls, and The Suitcase Kid.*

The Tales of Olga da Polga
Michael Bond
ISBN-13: 978-0-19-275130-0
ISBN-10: 0-19-275130-1

Olga da Polga is no ordinary guinea-pig. She's a very special guinea-pig indeed . . . and she knows it!

From the minute Olga arrives at her new home, she gathers all the other animals in the garden around and starts telling them exciting tales about all the wild and wonderful adventures she's had. Sometimes the other animals aren't sure whether to believe her or not—but surely Olga wouldn't be making them up, would she?

Olga Meets Her Match
Michael Bond
ISBN-13: 978-0-19-275132-4
ISBN-10: 0-19-275132-8

The Sawdust family decide Olga needs a holiday, so off she goes for a break by the sea. During her stay she becomes friends with Boris, a Russian guinea-pig, and is surprised to discover that Boris has as many stories to tell as she does!